DANGEROUS WATERS

LANTERN BEACH MYSTERIES, BOOK 4

CHRISTY BARRITT

COMPLETE BOOK LIST

Squeaky Clean Mysteries:
  #1 Hazardous Duty
  #2 Suspicious Minds
  #2.5 It Came Upon a Midnight Crime (novella)
  #3 Organized Grime
  #4 Dirty Deeds
  #5 The Scum of All Fears
  #6 To Love, Honor and Perish
  #7 Mucky Streak
  #8 Foul Play
  #9 Broom & Gloom
  #10 Dust and Obey
  #11 Thrill Squeaker
  #11.5 Swept Away (novella)
  #12 Cunning Attractions
  #13 Cold Case: Clean Getaway
  #14 Cold Case: Clean Sweep
  #15 Cold Case: Clean Break

#16 Cleans to an End

While You Were Sweeping, A Riley Thomas Spinoff

The Sierra Files:

#1 Pounced

#2 Hunted

#3 Pranced

#4 Rattled

The Gabby St. Claire Diaries (a Tween Mystery series):

#1 The Curtain Call Caper

#2 The Disappearing Dog Dilemma

#3 The Bungled Bike Burglaries

The Worst Detective Ever

#1 Ready to Fumble

#2 Reign of Error

#3 Safety in Blunders

#4 Join the Flub

#5 Blooper Freak

#6 Flaw Abiding Citizen

#7 Gaffe Out Loud

#8 Joke and Dagger

#9 Wreck the Halls

#10 Glitch and Famous

#11 Not on My Botch

Raven Remington

Relentless

Holly Anna Paladin Mysteries:
#1 Random Acts of Murder
#2 Random Acts of Deceit
#2.5 Random Acts of Scrooge
#3 Random Acts of Malice
#4 Random Acts of Greed
#5 Random Acts of Fraud
#6 Random Acts of Outrage
#7 Random Acts of Iniquity

Lantern Beach Mysteries
#1 Hidden Currents
#2 Flood Watch
#3 Storm Surge
#4 Dangerous Waters
#5 Perilous Riptide
#6 Deadly Undertow

Lantern Beach Romantic Suspense
#1 Tides of Deception
#2 Shadow of Intrigue
#3 Storm of Doubt
#4 Winds of Danger
#5 Rains of Remorse
#6 Torrents of Fear

Lantern Beach P.D.
#1 On the Lookout
#2 Attempt to Locate
#3 First Degree Murder

#2 Dylan

#3 Maddox

#4 Titus

Lantern Beach Christmas

Silent Night

Crime á la Mode

#1 Dead Man's Float

#2 Milkshake Up

#3 Bomb Pop Threat

#4 Banana Split Personalities

Beach Bound Books and Beans Mysteries

#1 Bound by Murder

#2 Bound by Disaster

#3 Bound by Mystery

#4 Bound by Trouble

#5 Bound by Mayhem

Vanishing Ranch

#1 Forgotten Secrets

#2 Necessary Risk

#3 Risky Ambition

#4 Deadly Intent

#5 Lethal Betrayal

#6 High Stakes Deception

#7 Fatal Vendetta

#8 Troubled Tidings

#9 Narrow Escape

The Sidekick's Survival Guide

#1 The Art of Eavesdropping

#2 The Perks of Meddling

#3 The Exercise of Interfering

#4 The Practice of Prying

#5 The Skill of Snooping

#6 The Craft of Being Covert

Saltwater Cowboys

#1 Saltwater Cowboy

#2 Breakwater Protector

#3 Cape Corral Keeper

#4 Seagrass Secrets

#5 Driftwood Danger

#6 Unwavering Security

Beach House Mysteries

#1 The Cottage on Ghost Lane

#2 The Inn on Hanging Hill

#3 The House on Dagger Point

School of Hard Rocks Mysteries

#1 The Treble with Murder

#2 Crime Strikes a Chord

#3 Tone Death

Carolina Moon Series

#1 Home Before Dark

#2 Gone By Dark

#3 Wait Until Dark

    #4 Light the Dark
    #5 Taken By Dark

Suburban Sleuth Mysteries:
    Death of the Couch Potato's Wife

Fog Lake Suspense:
    #1 Edge of Peril
    #2 Margin of Error
    #3 Brink of Danger
    #4 Line of Duty
    #5 Legacy of Lies
    #6 Secrets of Shame
    #7 Refuge of Redemption

Cape Thomas Series:
    #1 Dubiosity
    #2 Disillusioned
    #3 Distorted

Standalone Romantic Mystery:
    The Good Girl

Suspense:
    Imperfect
    The Wrecking

Sweet Christmas Novella:
    Home to Chestnut Grove

Standalone Romantic-Suspense:

Keeping Guard

The Last Target

Race Against Time

Ricochet

Key Witness

Lifeline

High-Stakes Holiday Reunion

Desperate Measures

Hidden Agenda

Mountain Hideaway

Dark Harbor

Shadow of Suspicion

The Baby Assignment

The Cradle Conspiracy

Trained to Defend

Mountain Survival

Dangerous Mountain Rescue

Nonfiction:

Characters in the Kitchen

Changed: True Stories of Finding God through Christian Music (out of print)

The Novel in Me: The Beginner's Guide to Writing and Publishing a Novel (out of print)

PROLOGUE

18 WEEKS EARLIER

"I'VE GOT AN ASSIGNMENT FOR YOU." Raul Sanders's words blasted an arctic chill across the small room.

With more than a touch of trepidation, Cady Matthews stepped closer, carefully concealing her apprehension. She'd been called—summoned, more like it—into Raul Sanders's lair, the place where he served like an evil king over his foot soldiers. Even the leather chair he sat in acted as a throne, and his gold teeth were his crown.

She licked her lips and glanced beside her, noting that Orion had shown up also. He was one of Raul's right-hand men. Raul's other sidekick, Sloan, had disappeared two days ago, and no one had heard from him. Cady had a sickening feeling she knew exactly what had happened to the man.

Raul had killed him . . . or he'd had his men do it for him.

"What's this assignment?" Cady finally asked.

"You and Orion need to go do a job for me. You're the only two I trust."

She swallowed hard, not liking the sound of that. Raul's jobs were always bad news, and another name for committing a crime—against the government and against herself.

But Cady, an undercover detective, was here for a reason—to gain Raul's trust. So she did what she had to. "Sure. What do you need?"

He flipped a picture from his pocket and held it up. "You need to kill him."

Her stomach sank and squeezed and tried to heave as possibilities raced through her mind. "Who is he?"

"Reginald. He's someone I once trusted." Darkness rolled over his features. "He was one of us, but he left and joined the Blood Brotherhood. Betrayed us. Broke my heart. No one breaks my heart. No one."

The last lines were a threat more than a signal of grief. Again, it went back to loyalty.

Loyalty given was a gift. Loyalty broken was a curse —a curse the perpetrator would pay for dearly. Cady would be wise to keep that in mind.

Orion shifted and folded his bulky arms over his chest, looking more like a bodyguard than Raul's minion. "How do you want the job done?"

The brawny man was over six feet tall, with light brown skin and stark black hair that was shaved on the sides and hung long and straight on top. His hands were constantly fisted, and he didn't know how to smile.

In other words, he scared the dickens out of Cady.

"I'll let you two figure it out." Raul pulled out another piece of paper. "Here's his address. Reginald won't know you're coming. We've got to send a message loud and clear that no one walks away from DH-7. You got it?"

Cady nodded, covering her fear for the assignment and her repulsion for the man with her cold aloofness— a mask she had perfected. "Got it."

"Don't disappoint me." Raul locked gazes with her, his eyes holding a challenge.

"Wouldn't dream of it."

"And I want it done tonight."

Tonight? That didn't give Cady much time to think things through, to figure out a better solution. It definitely didn't give her time to call Samuel Stephens, her task force leader and the one who could pull the plug on this if necessary.

"We got this, boss." Orion glared at Cady. "At least, I do."

"Don't discount me, Const." That was Cady's nickname for him—Constellation. She hadn't given him a nickname as a means of affection. No, she abhorred the man. But she was here on a mission that required attempting, at least, to develop comradery with the man.

"I'd rather work with anyone else," Orion snapped back, his top lip rising in disgust.

"Quiet, you two." Raul's voice sliced through the air. "You're like siblings. Like Cain and Abel."

"Cain killed Abel," Cady muttered.

A glimmer of . . . something . . . filled Raul's gaze. "So you know your Bible. Then you also know that even though Cain may have been a killer, he helped father generations to come."

What did that mean? Was he saying Orion would lead the gang? That they planned to take over the world? Maybe even just a generation?

She didn't know, and it didn't matter at the moment.

Cady had bigger issues to face right now. Like how to complete this assignment without losing her soul.

CHAPTER
ONE

TODAY'S GOALS: NONE. JUST
LIVE AND TREASURE THE TIME
WITH THE PEOPLE I'M WITH.
MAYBE COLLECT A SEASHELL
OR TWO.

CASSIDY LIVINGSTON SMILED as she watched Ty Chambers. With the sun rising behind him as he stoked the small bonfire, he looked like he could grace one of those touristy beach brochures that were as plentiful in the area as the constant waves. He was fit, handsome, and looked like he belonged in this land of sun and sand.

Ty was showing off his cooking skills by making a rugged yet gourmet breakfast for the two of them. Some kind of whitefish cooked on a cedar plank resting on the flames. The savory aroma mixed with the salty air smelled heavenly.

On another piece of wood sat two bagels. Some cream cheese and fruit were in a wooden tray beside everything. If Ty's retreat center didn't work out, maybe he could become a personal chef.

"It looks delicious," Cassidy said.

Even though it was warm outside—typical for

August—she'd worn her favorite sweatshirt and jeans. Mornings and evenings could still be chilly, despite the scorching heat during the day. She sat on a striped blanket provided by Ty, drinking coffee from the travel mug he'd also provided.

He'd thought of everything.

"Conditions have to be just right to cook like this," Ty said, turning the fish with a metal spatula. Smoke billowed up, and the crackle of the fire almost sounded like applause. "That's why this had to happen this morning. We rarely have days where the wind is at less than seven knots."

He leaned toward the fire, absorbed in what he was doing. He'd had shoulder surgery a month ago, and he was recovering nicely. Cassidy almost couldn't tell he'd even had the operation, as far as recovery and ease of motion. All his physical therapy must be paying off.

Cassidy's eyes fastened on his broad shoulders, the rippling muscles on his broad back, and his face as the early morning sun bathed him in a golden glow. He was a sight to behold, and it wasn't just because of his good looks. No, it was who he was as a whole. The protector. The one who put others before himself. The only person who had the ability to make Cassidy forget her troubles.

Ty glanced back at her and did a double take. "Uh oh. Do I have something between my teeth?"

He sat back beside her, resting his arms against his bent knees as he waited for her answer. Birds circled overhead, crying out to be included in their moment.

Not a chance.

"No, nothing between your teeth." Cassidy looped her arm through his and leaned against his shoulder. "I was just thinking about how incredibly lucky I am."

"Why's that? Because you live on Lantern Beach?" His voice held that teasing tone Cassidy had come to crave.

"Well, that's one reason." She stared at the fire and the Atlantic Ocean beyond it as the waves lapped onto the sandy shores. "But it's mostly that I get free ice cream as one of my job perks."

"Is that right?"

"Uh um. And . . . well, because I'm here with you."

"You're getting pretty good at this sweet talk thing." Ty nudged her playfully.

"Well, it's hard, but I'm trying." Funny how her voice seemed to smile when she talked to him.

"It's hard, huh?" He turned toward Cassidy, his tone low, husky, and mischievous.

"You can be impossible sometimes." Cassidy raised her head from his shoulder in order to look him in the eye—in his twinkling eyes.

"Well, I'm glad you're never impossible."

She let out a short, blunt chuckle. "Me too."

Ty's eyes lost the amused look, and his gaze turned serious. He reached for Cassidy and pulled her close before skimming his hand down the side of her face. He'd never told her he loved her, but the look in his eyes right now said it all.

He was falling for Cassidy just as quickly as Cassidy

was falling for him. They'd officially been a couple for a month and had enjoyed lots of time together here on this beach, just relishing each other's company, friendship, and kisses.

During the day, Ty worked on transforming his cottage from a 900-square-foot bungalow into a 3,000-square-foot retreat center. With the help of his friend Austin, they'd figured out a way to rework the bones of the place to accommodate more people by creating an open floor plan and adding a new wing onto the back. Eventually they'd add a couple of guest houses on the property as well. He was remodeling it in order to start Hope House, a retreat center for injured veterans.

Meanwhile, Cassidy sold ice cream from her truck, Elsa. On Sundays, they went to church together, and during other free time they played volleyball with their friends or took walks along the majestic shoreline. Ty had even been teaching her how to surf fish.

There wasn't anything Cassidy would change about her life here.

Well, maybe one thing.

The fact that she couldn't tell Ty the truth about who she really was. Cady Matthews, Seattle detective, who'd infiltrated a dangerous gang. She'd killed the gang's leader, Raul Sanders. As a result, she had been forced into hiding. A million-dollar bounty had been placed on her head, and gang members across the country were now clamoring to find her and make her an example to anyone else who dared defy them.

All of that wasn't too much for someone to swallow . . . was it?

Ty slowly pressed his lips to Cassidy's. As he pulled away, his face remained close to hers, and he caressed her jaw.

Often what's simple is what's ultimately important.

Cassidy relished the advice from the Day-at-a-Glance calendar that used to belong to her best friend, Lucy. But, before she could savor the advice too long, there was something she had to say.

"Kujo is trying to eat the bagels," she whispered.

"What?"

"Kujo." She nodded toward the dog.

Ty snapped out of the moment and turned toward his golden retriever just as the dog snatched a bagel from the tray.

"What do you think you're doing, dog?" Ty shooed him away, and the dog happily bounded down the beach with his bounty.

"I'd say he's being smart."

"Well, you're always on Kujo's side. But maybe it was good timing because I think the fish is ready." He wiped his hands on a towel before using the spatula to finish making their breakfast. Bagel with cream cheese and smoked fish with fruit on the side.

It smelled—and looked—divine.

Ty presented her plate to her, watching closely as she tried her first bite.

The smoky, creamy flavor of the fish and cheese burst to life on her taste buds. "This is actually good."

"You doubted me?" He looked mockingly offended.

"I've gotta say that between you and Lisa, my palate has expanded in recent months. To think I used to be addicted to salads."

"A Texas girl who likes salads?"

"Yeah, well that was the old Cassidy." She remembered the life she'd left behind—how empty it had felt. And it wasn't just because of salads. "I like the new version a lot better."

They ate in silence for a few minutes until Ty cleared his throat. "So, I have an ulterior motive for fixing breakfast this morning. I wanted to tell you something."

"What's that?" Cassidy ate her last bite and put her plate on the ground, then wiped her mouth with a napkin Ty provided. Again, he'd thought of everything. He always did.

"I got that grant from Alpha Tech that you told me about."

Cassidy's heart lurched into her throat. It was her dad's company. Telling Ty about the grant program had been a risky move, but Cassidy knew exactly what her dad was looking for, and she'd helped guide him as he wrote the proposal. Her father handpicked the grant recipients himself.

Nothing about that process should trigger anyone to look for her here in Lantern Beach. There was no way they could link Ty and this grant back to her. No way.

She ordered her heart to slow and smiled up at Ty. "That's fantastic news."

"It means I'll be able to put my plan in motion. I've

just been working on things as I have the money. But with this check . . . I'll be able to work steady and hard until the project is complete."

Cassidy squeezed his hand. "I'm so happy for you, Ty. I know how important this is to you."

"There's nothing I want more than to have you beside me when this all comes to completion."

She looked away, her heart twisting into knots. She pictured that day. When would it be? A year from now? Longer? Either way, according to her timeline, she would be gone. As much as she tried to convince herself this arrangement could last forever, she knew what her reality was. Her life was back—not in Texas—but in Seattle.

"We've talked about this." Her throat ached as she said the words. "Day by day, right?"

It was a stipulation of their relationship. They were going to enjoy each moment together without any pressure about the future. So far, that had worked to perfection.

Ty reached for her hand. "I know. I do, Cassidy. I'm not pushing you. I just . . . I just want to let you know how much you mean to me. The idea of you not being in my future? It makes my world feel lopsided."

"I feel the same way." And she did. Unequivocally.

And that was what made this all the harder.

Ty leaned in for another kiss, but Cassidy's phone buzzed, interrupting the moment. She glanced at the screen and let out a sigh.

"That's right. I have a meeting."

"With who?" Ty asked.

"Serena." Serena worked for Cassidy part-time, helping with the ice cream route. But, in order to make ends meet, the college student also worked at her aunt's produce stand and as a beat reporter for the island newspaper.

He made a face. "Why doesn't she just come here? What's so important?"

"The moment I understand Serena is the moment dolphins come ashore and do the hula." Cassidy loved Serena, but the girl was a case study in personality disorders. Every time Cassidy saw her, she was dressed in a different style in a daily effort to "find herself."

Ty chuckled. "I can't argue with that. If you have to go, you have to go."

"She said it was important when she called last night. Otherwise, I'd stay here with you." Cassidy gave him another quick kiss. "But I'll see you later, okay?"

"Sure thing."

She stood and headed back toward her place. But first, she glanced over her shoulder, drinking in the sight of Ty on the beach one more time. "The fish was delicious."

"Thanks. The company wasn't bad either."

She smiled. No, the company had been perfect.

———

Cassidy walked along the boardwalk with a cup of iced coffee in hand. She'd arrived a few minutes early, so she'd indulged at her favorite coffee shop. It wasn't Seattle-worthy java, but it wasn't bad.

She was supposed to meet Serena here, on one of the benches facing the ocean and normally utilized by vacationers who wanted to soak in the million-dollar view. Conversations were always easier over a cup of coffee. That was her excuse right now, anyway.

She lingered near the spot a moment, her heart swelling with contentment.

The past month had been amazing. No mysteries. No fear of blowing her cover. Only good times living the simple life.

Living a life where she constantly looked over her shoulder had become the norm. It wasn't one she liked. But slowly, Cassidy's new persona was burying the person she used to be and making her forget her brisk, busy life as a big-city detective.

Back then, everything had revolved around work and getting ahead, which made for twenty-hour shifts and no social life. She hadn't realized what she was missing until she came to Lantern Beach. Even her assumed name was beginning to feel as comfortable as her favorite sweater.

"Cassidy!" someone called.

She looked up in time to see Serena Lavania headed her way, a file in hand and a bright smile on her face. Today the college student was dressed in some kind of ode to eighties punk rock, with an off-the-shoulder short-sleeve sweatshirt, a bright pink streak in her hair, and thirtyish bangles on her wrists.

The girl otherwise looked normal, with her slight build, bright eyes, and long, dark hair. She was visiting from Michigan for the summer, and she always made life more interesting, to say the least.

"What's going on?" Cassidy took the last sip of her coffee and tossed the cup into a nearby trash bin. Then she stripped off her sweatshirt—careful not to displace the "Salt Life" baseball cap on her head. She had no time to fix her hair this morning, and the humidity would have ruined any work she did anyway. She tied the shirt around her waist, ready to face the heat.

"Thanks for meeting with me," Serena said. "Sorry for the urgency, but I'm on deadline. I'm doing an article on the ten most important news stories of the summer. Your name came up in three of them."

Cassidy's throat tightened. "Is that right?"

Serena opened her manila folder. There wasn't much news around here, so Cassidy had been mentioned multiple times. "Yeah, but it's the craziest thing. Did you know that every time your picture is in the paper, no one can see your face?"

Cassidy glanced at the newspaper clippings Serena held out. The one on top was from when Cassidy had been given an award for her part in taking down a drug ring. Conveniently, when the picture had been taken, the wind had blown her hair in her face.

In other photos her hat was pulled down low, or she had sunglasses on, or someone's shoulder blocked her, or she'd just happened to look away.

No, Cassidy couldn't risk her face showing up in a

publication. DH-7 might be a street gang, but they had money and resources. They could hire someone to use software that would scan faces on the World Wide Web until they found a match and located her.

"You really can't see my face, can you? Isn't that funny?" Cassidy was thankful she wore sunglasses now so Serena couldn't see her unease.

"Anyway, it looks like you're the big winner when it comes to this summer's top stories," Serena said. "Which brings me to why I wanted to meet with you."

"I'm not following."

Serena pulled a camera from her bag. "I was hoping to get a picture of you. A better one. And I have to say —you've solved a murder, busted a drug ring, and helped three human-trafficking victims—you're like a rock star."

"Hardly. You really shouldn't run that article now. You should wait until there's an end-of-the-year edition." By the end of the year, the trial should be over, and publicity wouldn't matter. Right now, it did. It *really* did.

"Don't be ridiculous. This will make for great news. All the stories about you make the other ones look lame. For real. I mean, there's a fishing competition. Boring. The best floats in the Fourth of July parade. Yawn. The tourist whose foot got stuck while parasailing. Not as boring, but still."

"But that's a lot more fun than anything I'm involved with."

Serena didn't seem to hear her. "Maybe we should

just do the top three stories of the summer, and then we can avoid all the boring stuff. Besides, I'll be gone by the end of the year. I *love* bylines. Well, I love *my* byline."

Cassidy needed to convince Serena that this was a bad idea.

She opened her mouth, about to offer unsolicited advice.

But she stopped cold.

A figure weaving in and out of the crowds in the distance caught her eye.

Was that . . .

No, it couldn't be.

She squinted, trying to soak in the details.

But maybe it was.

Cassidy quickly turned her back and ducked behind the wooden post of a pergola. Her heart thumped out of control.

That man looked exactly like Orion. One of Raul's leaders. And a man who wanted to kill Cassidy, all in the name of justice for DH-7.

Had they found her?

CHAPTER
TWO

"ARE YOU OKAY?" Serena tilted her head at Cassidy and squinted with scrutiny. "You look pale. Do you really hate publicity that much?"

"Maybe I'm coming down with something," Cassidy muttered, the article the least of her worries right now. She glanced back again.

The man was still coming her way. He'd pass by her in the next three minutes, by her calculations.

Cassidy had to get out of here.

"Serena, don't run that article," she muttered. "And I hate having my picture taken."

"Okay . . . fine. It was just an idea." Serena's bottom lip jutted out in a pout.

"I just remembered something. I hate to cut this short, but I need to go."

"Are you sure you're okay?" Serena blinked in confusion and concern.

Cassidy nodded and waved a hand in the air,

hoping to alleviate the girl's concerns. Then she hurried down the sidewalk, away from Orion.

At the first open shop, Cassidy ducked inside and out of sight.

Her lungs squeezed, tight with anxiety. How had Orion found her? Was it really him?

She couldn't be sure. It could be someone who *looked* like him.

Yet, at first glance, Cassidy had felt certain. She had to trust her gut. There were times to play it safe, and times to take risks. Right now, surrounded by innocent bystanders, she chose to play it safe.

Cassidy feigned looking at some T-shirts as she peered out the window at the busy boardwalk outside. She waited, counting down the seconds until the man walked past.

Would Orion continue on? Or had he already seen Cassidy? Was he hunting her down now, preparing himself to confront her at the first chance?

She had no idea.

She knew the way he worked. Swiftly. Without conscience. With a devious plan.

Her heart pounded harder. Cassidy's gun was in her purse. She could use it if she had to.

"Can I help you?" a cracking pubescent voice came from behind her.

She glanced over her shoulder, and her stomach tightened. An annoying salesperson she'd encountered before leered at her. He was the most persistent teenager she'd ever met, and the last thing Cassidy wanted right now was to talk to him.

"I'm fine," Cassidy mumbled, returning her attention to the front window.

Orion—or whoever that man was—should be coming past any second.

"We've got some great specials," the boy continued.

"I'm okay." More tourists passed outside. But no Orion. Not yet.

"Maybe you'd like an aquatic frog?"

She needed to get rid of him. Now.

"There's a shoplifter on the other side of the store," she muttered. "He's stuffing things into his sweatshirt as we speak. You should go check him out before the manager blames you for not paying better attention."

Cassidy had glanced at the thief when she walked inside and noted him scoping out the place. Stopping him wasn't a battle she could fight right now. But if it got this salesclerk off her back, then great.

"What . . . really . . ." Without saying another word, the clerk disappeared.

Thank goodness.

And just in time. Orion strode past the window.

Cassidy squinted again.

Was that Orion? Or was she paranoid?

The man looked like him. Kind of.

Cassidy's heart raced. Her lungs tightened.

Her entire body was poised to either fight or take flight.

But then he passed. Kept walking. Didn't look back.

She'd only ever seen Orion dressed like a gang-banger with baggy jeans, too much jewelry, and that defiant look he constantly wore. The man who'd just passed had the same dark hair and broad build. But he was dressed in gray shorts and a black top. Both looked pressed and clean. He wore sandals, and his short hair was combed stylishly.

The man physically shared Orion's characteristics, but everything else didn't match. His vibe was different.

What did that mean?

Cassidy wasn't sure. But she wasn't going to stay here and figure it out either. No, because if Orion found her, it wasn't just Cassidy who'd be in danger. So would everyone she loved.

And that wasn't okay.

———

Panic threatened to seize every part of Cassidy. She pulled up to her cottage, rushed up the stairs, and flew into her house.

Did Orion know where she lived? Was he headed here now? What would he do when he found her?

She threw some clothes into a bag, jamming them in with a punch.

How had the man managed to locate her? Was it the grant? Had it somehow triggered something?

It didn't matter. Not right now.

What mattered—the only thing that mattered—was that she got out of here.

Cassidy had known there was a chance this time would come. She'd thought through the possibilities. Played them out in her head.

She'd just hoped none of them ever came to fruition.

Oh, dear Lord. Help me. Help the people I love. Keep them safe.

She moved from the bedroom into the kitchen. She grabbed a backpack and threw her guns inside, along with a few water bottles and all the cash she could find. She'd take her sedan for now, but she'd need to find a new car soon. Just to be safe.

That was all she had time to pack. She'd worry about the rest later. She could buy more clothes. More food. More toiletries. Maybe she'd dye her hair red. Cut it short. Go somewhere cold this time.

Her heart ached at the thought of it.

She didn't want to go anywhere else. Her heart was here in Lantern Beach.

Focus, Cassidy. This is bigger than you. Bigger than this town. Your happiness takes a backseat to your job.

That statement had never bothered her—until now.

All her focus had been on the bigger picture. The FBI needed her testimony to put these guys away for good. That was why it was so important she stay alive. That she put her life on hold in order to do the right thing.

The right thing.

She knew what that required of her. And she'd

known it would be difficult. *The right thing is sometimes the hardest thing. Do it anyway.*

Cassidy cast one last glance at her little home, and memories filled her. Memories of her friends eating here. Of people in need hiding out. Of quiet dinners with Ty, enjoying each other's company.

She could hardly swallow the idea of leaving.

Before Cassidy could talk herself out of it, she rushed out the door. It was best if she got out of here before anyone saw her. Before she could second-guess herself any more. Before she could talk herself out of doing what was necessary.

She scurried down the exterior stairway and threw her bags into the back seat of her sedan. She started to open the driver's side door when she glanced at Ty's place and paused.

The pang in her heart echoed through her entire body until she bent with pain.

Stay focused.

But more than anything she wanted to stay here.

You'll get everyone you love killed if you stay.

With that thought, she climbed into her sedan. Heartbreak was better than death. It might not seem like it initially, but people could recover from emotions. Death was permanent—here on this earth, at least.

Just as she was about to shut the door, someone called her name.

Cassidy froze and looked up.

Ty lumbered down the stairs from his place.

"Where are you rushing off to now? You already met

with Serena?" He sauntered to her car, his flip-flops smacking against the cement.

Cassidy realized he might see her bags in the back and quickly climbed out, trying to block him from the sight of them and any questions that would arise as a result.

Her heart ached, the pain nearly unbearable. This could be the last time they spoke. Cassidy could hardly stomach the thought. Ty had come to mean the world to her.

"I forgot something and had to come back for it," she said, her voice cracking. "No biggie."

"You seem different." He squinted and studied her face. "Frazzled or something."

"Do I? I just hate when I forget things." Cassidy looked up into his eyes and felt her resolve weakening.

She loved that face. Loved his warm, brown eyes and messy hair and defined jaw. Loved how his cheeks got scruffy and how sometimes he liked to wear cowboy boots on the beach. Loved the way he worked with his hands, leaving calluses that told stories of perseverance and hard work. How he loved his dog. How loyal he was to his friends.

Cassidy had never met anyone like Ty Chambers. And she never would again. But she had to do what she had to do.

Your happiness is secondary to the mission.

The thought caused a wave of bitterness to rise in her.

Spontaneously, Cassidy reached for Ty and drew

him close. She pressed her lips against his in a kiss she never wanted to stop. She never wanted to let go. Never wanted the moment to end.

But it did. Of course.

"What was that for?" Ty's voice sounded low and intimate as he studied her face, his hands still draped at her waist.

"Can't I kiss you just because?"

"It almost felt like," his gaze jerked behind her and his eyes narrowed, "a goodbye kiss. Are those your bags in the back of the car? Are you leaving, Cassidy?"

Cassidy's blood pressure surged until her ears roared with an almost static sound. "Why would you ask that?"

As soon as the words left her mouth, regret filled her. Ty wasn't stupid, and she didn't want to treat him like he was. He deserved better, especially after everything he'd done for her.

"What's going on, Cassidy?" His gaze hardened. "Talk to me."

She licked her lips. The less he knew, the better. For his own sake. "It's complicated."

"I understand complicated. I went to war." His expression turned stony.

Tears sprang to Cassidy's eyes as all her emotions came to the surface. That was the last thing she needed. Her emotions . . . they'd only make her weak. That was what her dad had always told her.

"I can't." Her voice cracked. "I just can't."

The hardness in his eyes turned cold. "You still don't trust me."

"It's not like that."

"I'd say it is."

"Ty . . ." She could feel the chasm between them growing and expanding by the second. And it was all her fault.

She'd created this divide. She should have never let herself get so close. Yet she didn't regret it. The past month had been the best of her life.

Which only made this moment more painful.

Ty stepped away, his hands on his hips, and his muscles bristled and tight. The ache in Cassidy's chest cavity built with pressure until she felt like she might throw up.

But what else could she say? How could she begin to explain the unexplainable? She already knew the answer. She couldn't.

"Will I see you again?" he asked.

Yes, say yes! But would he? Where was life going to take her? And for how long? What if the trial got delayed again? She could be caught up in this for a long time. Years.

"I . . . I don't know."

He nodded stiffly, his good mood evaporating like a summer rain shower on a ninety-degree day. "Have a safe trip then."

"Ty . . ."

He pressed his lips together and shook his head. The questions in his eyes were loud and clear, as was the heavy silence while he gathered his thoughts. "I don't know what else to say, Cassidy. I can't force you to make the decision that I want."

"There's so much more to this." She hadn't meant to say that, but it was out there now.

"What's that even mean?" Frustration tinged his words.

With each minute that passed, Orion could be drawing closer. Ty could be in more danger. Yet she wanted to stay. To explain. To start over.

"You're not going to tell me, are you?" Ty asked.

"Ty . . ." Cassidy licked her lips, caught between the proverbial rock and hard place. The position just might crush her.

"Go," he said.

But the dull sound of his voice broke her heart. She'd hurt him. How could she have ever thought things would end differently? She'd been a fool to ever get involved with Ty in the first place.

From the very beginning, she'd known the ending. But that didn't make this any easier.

Cassidy climbed in the car before her defenses weakened too much. And then she pulled out of the driveway, preparing herself to start a new life in a new place that already felt empty and incomplete without Ty by her side.

CHAPTER
THREE

TEARS RAN DOWN Cassidy's cheeks as she reached the end of the gravel lane beyond her cottage and started out of town. To the ferry. To another island. Where she would catch another ferry to another island. Eventually she'd get away from here. Away from Orion.

Away from Ty.

A small sob escaped at the thought.

Focus, Cassidy. Focus.

Once on the ferry, she'd call Samuel Stephens, her one and only contact while undercover. He might shed some insight on where to go. He'd secure a new identity for her and maybe a place to live.

Then she'd start over. Again. Remember not to get too close to anyone this time.

A hollow feeling expanded in her gut. Leaving might not feel so devastating if she hadn't experienced the satisfaction of a full life—a life with happiness and friends and . . . love.

Ty . . . an image of him slammed into her mind with enough force that she flinched right there in the driver's seat. The ache inside her was so strong that she nearly felt beside herself, like someone else was driving this car out of town and away from everything she held dear.

"I can't leave him," she whispered, unable to get a deep breath.

But she had to.

The two thoughts warred inside Cassidy until she felt as if she might throw up. It wasn't supposed to be this hard. This agonizing. Then again, she'd never planned on meeting Ty. Of falling for him. Of having her life turned upside down in the best way possible.

Cassidy's grip on the steering wheel tightened as she replayed their conversation. The hurt in his eyes. The invisible wall that had shot up, separating them not only physically but emotionally. A wall created by pain. Created by her.

None of this was fair—to her. But mostly to Ty. Cassidy was leaving him with questions he might never have answers to. Leaving him to struggle. To wonder if it was him. To wrestle with the unknown.

Just like what had happened with his ex-fiancée.

Renee had left his life in shambles, a mere rubble of what it had been, like a war-torn town.

Now Cassidy was doing the same thing.

You have to live with your choices for the rest of your life.

At that thought, Cassidy hit the brakes. She jerked

the wheel to the left. Her car fishtailed right there on the highway until coming to a dramatic stop.

She eased from the center of the road and onto the nearest residential street. With her car in Park, she tried to gather herself. Her heart pounded into her chest, and her lungs heaved in each breath.

She couldn't do this. She couldn't leave without an explanation. Couldn't make Ty live the rest of his life—or even the next few months—with the questions he'd wrestle with.

Cassidy's instincts told her she could trust Ty. She knew that beyond a doubt.

She'd grown up hardly trusting anyone. Trust always came with a price—usually betrayal, the gut-wrenching realization that someone had been using her because of her father's position of power or because of her family's money.

But Ty . . . he wasn't like that. He'd asked nothing of Cassidy, except for her to be . . . her.

Cassidy threw her car in reverse and backed out. She was going to abandon all the rules for a minute, hoping and praying the fallout would be worth it.

She wasn't leaving without making things right.

That was the only choice she could live with.

A few minutes later, Cassidy pulled into Ty's driveway. She parked and rushed upstairs to his place. He answered on the first knock, that hard expression borne of hurt still etched on his face. But surprise—and maybe hope—had inched into his gaze also.

"You're back," he said.

Cassidy just had to say this—get it all out—rather than try her hand at being eloquent. "You're the best thing that's ever happened to me, Ty Chambers, and I can't leave here without telling you what's going on."

He leaned against the doorframe, still standoffish. "I'd love to listen."

"We can't talk here." Cassidy glanced down the beach, half expecting to see Orion headed this way. She didn't. That didn't mean the man wasn't close. "It's . . . it's not safe."

"Not safe?" Ty squinted, as if struggling to comprehend her meaning.

Anyone would. And this was just getting started. When he heard Cassidy's larger-than-life story, she had no idea how he would react. It would be hard for even the most seasoned veteran to comprehend.

"I can't explain here."

He unfolded his arms and nodded slowly, thoughtfully. "I know just where we can go to talk privately."

"Thank you. Could we take your truck?"

He nodded, but his gaze was still full of questions. "Sure."

"And Kujo?" Cassidy couldn't live with herself if something happened to his dog. "We should take Kujo."

"Of course."

She still felt lightheaded at the possibilities before her. But she had no choice other than seeing this through to completion.

For better or worse.

Cassidy prayed it was for the better.

———

Ty gripped the steering wheel of his truck, trying not to ask the hundreds of questions racing through his mind. He'd wait until he got to his destination and he could look Cassidy in the eye. Some conversations required no distractions.

One truth remained: whatever it was that Cassidy needed to tell him, she was terrified like Ty had never seen her before.

And Cassidy might be the jumpy type, but she wasn't fearful. In fact, sometimes she could be downright fierce. Those facts only made all of this more confounding and worrisome.

Thank goodness, she'd come back. Because for the five minutes she'd been gone, Ty had felt like he'd lost everything. He'd realized that his world would never again be the same without Cassidy in it. He'd fallen hard, and he'd fallen fast.

Ty glanced at Cassidy as the windswept landscape blurred past and noted how pale her skin was as she stared out the window. Her breathing was shallow. Apprehension lined her rigid back and shoulders.

He reached over and laced his fingers through hers. Cassidy squeezed back but remained silent and stoic. A slight tremor shook her hand.

Ty had suspected for a while there was more to her story. About why she came to Lantern Beach. An abusive ex. A crime she'd unwillingly been a part of. Whatever danger she ran from, it caused her to keep a hidden stash of guns. He'd known she would open up in her own time.

He'd never imagined it like this.

Fifteen minutes later, after driving through town and then through the wooded outskirts of the island's southern end, he pulled up to the old lighthouse. He'd been helping their friend Austin restore the place over the past few months. It was secluded out here, but Ty would spot anyone who approached. Which made it perfect for whatever Cassidy had to share.

He hoped.

Wordlessly, they climbed from his truck, Cassidy grabbing her backpack like it was a lifeline. He suspected, based on the weight and bulk of the bag, that her guns were inside.

With Kujo on their heels, they stepped into the light-keeper's quarters.

He'd wanted to bring Cassidy here sometime and show her around. She'd love this building that was full of history and intrigue. If these walls could talk, they'd have stories that were movie-worthy.

But this wasn't the time.

With no AC, the humidity curled around them, blanketing them in a heavy, weighted heat. With it came the scent of age, of a space that had been closed up too long. Undercurrents of sawdust and lacquer floated through the air, mixing with the scent of the ocean, which roared outside.

Ty led Cassidy to the couch that had been left years ago by the last family who'd acted as caretakers. He sat her down, not bothering to apologize for the cloud of dust that rose from the cushions as he lowered himself beside her.

"Talk to me, Cassidy," he encouraged.

She didn't break eye contact. No, she reached up and caressed his face, her eyes saying what words couldn't: she cared about him. Her sun-kissed face pulled tight with anxiety. Her hair, normally around her shoulders in carefree waves, was yanked back and hidden under a baseball cap.

It didn't matter what she wore or how she did her hair. She was flat-out the most beautiful woman Ty had ever met, inside and out.

"I didn't factor you into my plan." Cassidy's voice cracked with emotion as she stared at him, storms raging in her gaze.

"What plan, Cassidy?" She wasn't making any sense.

"The plan was for me to hide out here until I went back to Seattle to testify."

All Ty could hear was his heartbeat in his ears. What had Cassidy just said? Had he heard correctly?

Testify. Hide out. Seattle.

That was a long way from being an interior designer in one of the smallest towns in Texas.

"Are you in witness protection?" Was that what she was trying to tell him? Was that what all this was about?

Cassidy shook her head, squeezing her eyes shut as if she struggled to find the words. "No, I guess I should start at the beginning."

Ty's breath hitched as he prepared himself for whatever she was about to say. He prayed he'd have the right words, the right reaction. That he could be the man Cassidy needed him to be right now.

She licked her lips, and her gaze found his. The depths of emotion in her eyes nearly stopped his heart.

"My name is actually Cady Matthews." Her voice almost sounded robotic. "I'm a detective from Seattle, and I went undercover, infiltrating a dangerous gang. DH-7."

This was almost too much for Ty to comprehend. Cassidy wasn't her real name? Yet the detective piece cleared up so many questions: her ability to solve crimes. The guns. The way she interacted with life itself.

But DH-7? They were notorious. Dangerous. Deadly. Not a group of people you wanted to mess with, to say the least, even as a trained law enforcement officer.

She rubbed her hands on her jeans. "While I was undercover, I got the information I needed to complete my mission, and I was about to leave." Her voice quivered. "But before I could, the leader of the gang, Raul Sanders, caught me. He was about to kill me."

Ty grabbed her hand and squeezed it, hoping the small act might give her the strength to continue.

She squeezed her lips together, and her gaze glazed over, like she was going back to a different time and place. "But in a strange turn of events, I found a baseball, threw it at his chest, and it stopped his heart on contact."

"Commotio Cordis . . ." he muttered.

Not only was it a medical condition, it was also the nickname given to an urban folk hero, of sorts. Commotio Cordis was all the rage in underground circles. Some kids had even created comics about her, hailing her as a savior.

"That's me, though by no doing of my own." She frowned. "I moved to a safe house in Washington, but the gang found me. That's when we suspected there was someone on the inside working for them. It's the only way they could have located me. I managed to get out of the safe house alive, but I realized I had to get far away."

Ty pictured it playing out and used every bit of his self-control not to flinch at the thought of everything Cassidy had experienced. Right now, he needed to give his all to this conversation.

"So you came here to Lantern Beach?"

She nodded, her face and muscles still stiff. "My contact got the house for me, and he bought Elsa. My only mission was to lie low and hide until the trial."

"Something spooked you today, though?" He bristled at the thought. At everything he'd just learned. At the secret identity Cassidy—or should he call her Cady? —had been living under.

"I thought I saw Orion, one of Raul's right-hand men." She licked her lips, her wide eyes meeting his again. "You may have heard there's a one-million-dollar bounty on my head for whoever kills me."

Grief—and anger—ripped through him at the thought of anyone hurting her at all, but especially for profit. "I do remember that."

Cassidy reached up and stroked his cheek again, a tear rolling down her own. "Listen, I don't have time to play the dating game right now or to watch my words for fear of saying too much too soon."

"I've never liked games." His heart pounded harder.

"Ty Chambers, I care about you. I don't want to get you killed. That's why I need to leave."

Ty's heart lurched at the sincerity in her words. He felt the same way. And, while hearing those words leave her lips both thrilled him and tore him apart, he also realized the stakes here.

"Cassidy—Cady," he started.

"Just call me Cassidy. Please."

"Cassidy, if this guy realizes we're connected, I'm already a target, whether you're here or not."

She breathed out a small cry and lowered her head.

Ty pulled her closer until her head hit his chest. He wanted to squeeze tight and never let go. "Don't leave. Let me fight this battle with you."

"I'll never forgive myself if something happens to you."

"I've fought for my country and been willing to lay down my life. Of course, I'm going to fight for the woman I love."

She sucked in a breath, pulling back until her eyes

met his. Questions danced there . . . and maybe a little joy.

"Yes, I said it." He brushed a stray hair from her face. "I love you, Cassidy Livingston."

A smile finally cracked her face, along with a flood of emotion and a few more tears. "I love you too, Ty."

He tugged her closer and their lips met—the kiss almost desperate. Hungry. Speaking what words couldn't.

Kujo interrupted it with an incessant bark.

Ty glanced at Cassidy and saw her face pale again.

"Stay here," he ordered. He stood, going on alert.

Instead of obeying, Cassidy reached into her bag and withdrew a gun. "No way. Those are my monkeys, and this is my circus."

That was one way to put it.

She handed him a revolver, pulled out another gun for herself, and then followed him to the window.

Ty checked the weapon, saw it was loaded, and braced himself for the worst.

CASSIDY POSITIONED herself at the edge of the window, her gun raised and ready. "Do you see anything?"

Ty peered around the wall and shook his head. "No, nothing."

Kujo barked again, his motions more manic and agitated.

Cassidy gulped down a deep breath before turning toward the outside. She glanced out the glass, desperate for a glimpse of what was upsetting the canine. Desperate also to avoid a bullet.

Had Orion already found her? It didn't make sense. It was too soon. Too fast. Unless he'd been two steps ahead of her this whole time. That was a possibility.

She scanned the landscape outside—mostly shrubby trees against an otherwise barren stretch of land. Waves crashed in the background, their symphony loud enough to conceal any approaching visitors. Sand blew with the breeze, making everything appear hazy.

But she saw no one.

Ty nodded toward some trees. "Maybe it's just a squirrel."

"Maybe. I'll take a squirrel over a hit man any day."

Ty frowned. "We should stay here and keep watch, just in case."

Cassidy had seen the changing emotions on his face. The surprise mixed with concern and even anger. It would take him a while to fully process the extent of this. She wished she could do something to ease his worry, but she couldn't.

"What does this guy look like?" Ty asked.

Gripping her gun, Cassidy grabbed her phone from her back pocket with her free hand and did an Internet search. Some gang members wouldn't be caught dead on the web. Others liked the notoriety social media could bring. Orion fell into that second category.

He'd posted videos of himself making veiled threats and recorded gang initiations. He'd offered just enough incriminating evidence against himself that the police could arrest him—if they could find him. His ability to elude authorities and cover his tracks was his greatest strength.

She showed Ty Orion's image.

He blanched when he saw it. "Looks like a guy you don't want to cross."

"Coming from someone who fought terrorists in the Middle East, that about sums it up."

Cassidy knew, from their conversations, about the work he'd done as a SEAL. He'd faced down some of the world's most notorious, twisted criminals—mass murderers behind airplane bombings, chemical attacks, and public beheadings. He knew a thing or two about evil. He'd looked it in the eye.

"You can say that again." Ty ran a hand over his face.

Cassidy's insides went cold when she glanced at Orion's picture again. "He didn't flinch when it came to taking someone's life, Ty. I've never seen anything like it. The total absence of conscience."

"It's chilling, isn't it?"

She nodded, finding a strange comfort in the fact that Ty understood. She wished no one did and that evil didn't exist in the world. But it did. Her calling was to fight it.

She shifted before launching into her next piece of information. "The other thing is this. Two other women have died."

Ty squinted and studied her face. "What do you mean?"

Cassidy swallowed hard, hating the fact that the words she was about to say were true. Hating that she couldn't make things right or trade her own life for any of the innocent lives that had been lost. If only life worked that way.

"They were women who looked like me." Her throat felt like sand had been poured down it. "That bounty that DH-7 put out is a strong incentive for gang members across the country. For people who don't flinch when it comes to taking someone's life. Two people have already died because of me."

"It wasn't your fault." His voice pulled her from the brutal thoughts that tried to punch and bruise her.

"It feels like my fault. All of this does. I never meant to kill Raul. It was dumb luck, I suppose."

"You were trying to stay alive. You were fighting for your own life. Raul Sanders . . . I hate to say it, but the world is a better place without him."

She closed her eyes, fighting the memories and the guilt. "Maybe we should both leave." She glanced at Kujo. "All three of us, I mean."

"And what happens when Orion or another gang member finds you again?"

His words caused a shock of ice to fill Cassidy's heart. "Maybe he won't."

"If there is someone on the inside, then he will. Are you going to keep running for the next however many months? Years?"

"Movement is life. That's what my training officer always told me. You're more likely to stay alive if you keep moving."

"What happens after the trial, Cassidy?" Ty asked. "You think everyone in DH-7 is going to jail?"

"Of course not." That would be a Pollyanna way of thinking—and that was one thing Cassidy wasn't.

"They're not going to be happy that you put their leaders away—even killed one of them."

"No, they aren't." Her throat tightened. It wasn't pleasant to hear the truth, but it was necessary.

She hadn't had anyone to talk things through with for so long—anyone but Samuel. She only contacted him when absolutely necessary. He wasn't the type to act as a counselor *and* task force leader. It felt incredibly freeing to get everything off her chest, to not have to carry this alone.

But she hated that Ty was involved. Hated it.

"You aren't going to be able to resume your old life and assume these guys will never track you down," Ty said. "Believe me. I've been on some hit lists in the past. I know how they work."

Cassidy had thought it all through. She'd tried to, at least. But maybe, even though the analytical detective side of her cried out for truth and reasoning, the human side of her had dreamed of a better future for herself. A future where things were easier, happier.

"This guy probably wants the money for himself," Ty continued, glancing out the window again.

"That's a good guess."

"So maybe he came alone. Maybe no one else knows he's here."

"What are you suggesting, Ty?" Part of Cassidy didn't want to hear it. She wanted to stick with her original plan and leave. It was simple and easy.

Except that she'd abandon everything she'd grown to love.

"I'm suggesting you stand your ground, and you let us help."

"Us? Ty, no one else can know about this." A surge of panic rushed through her.

"It's going to take more than the two of us to finish this, Cass."

She swung her head back and forth. "That's a bad idea."

He raised a hand and palmed the air, motioning for her to calm down. "What if we include Mac?"

Mac, the former police chief in town, had become a good friend since Cassidy arrived. He was in his sixties, but he was spry, smart, and loyal. And he made Cassidy laugh—laughter was truly a gift.

"I'm not sure that's a good idea." A weight formed in her heart at the thought of pulling Mac into this. No one was supposed to know who she really was—not even Ty. Breaking protocol once? Maybe it was forgivable. Twice? She was asking for trouble.

Ty's gaze caught hers. "One thing I learned as a SEAL is the importance of a team that has your back."

"But . . ." It was so much more complicated than that.

"I know you don't want anyone to get hurt because of you. Mac knows what he's doing. He lives for stuff like this."

Cassidy couldn't argue with that. Yet she couldn't agree either.

She scanned the woods again, looking for any sign of Orion. Kujo resumed barking, causing her anxiety to creep higher.

Ty took her hand. "We're going to figure this out. But, for now, let's get away from the window."

He'd said *we*.

He was in this with her, whether she wanted him to be or not.

But the truth was, it felt so good to know she wasn't alone.

She squeezed his hand. As long as she was with him, that was all that mattered.

———

Ty pulled Cassidy through the living area, down the hallway, and past two bedrooms toward the back of the lightkeeper's residence.

"Where are we going?" she asked.

"You trust me, right?"

She didn't hesitate before saying, "I do."

"Just a little farther then." At the back of the building, he stopped at a thick door. As Ty opened it, more humidity crept out and darkness greeted them. To Ty, that was the smell of adventure.

"Is this . . . ?"

Ty turned back toward Cassidy and smiled. "It's the lighthouse tower."

"I've never climbed one before."

"Come on." He tugged her toward the iron staircase, anxious to see her face when they reached the top. "It's only eleven stories high."

"Only eleven stories, huh? Sounds like a walk in the

park."

"It's better than a gym membership."

"If you say so."

They skirted past the door. He called Kujo in behind them but commanded him to stay at the base of the structure. Then Ty pulled down a latch, barricading them in—for now. No one would get through this door.

"Is this safe?" Cassidy didn't sound fearful, only curious as she stared at the spiraling staircase.

"I wouldn't ask you to do this if it wasn't." He'd never purposefully put her in danger. "There are a few spots we'll have to watch out for. Believe me, I'll point them out well before we reach them."

There was a reason this place had closed to the public and sold to a private owner. Too much liability. Too much money to keep up the building. But to let something like this go to waste would be a shame.

"Let's go then," Cassidy said.

Ty began leading her up the narrow passage toward the top, sunlight streaming from the glass overhead illuminating their way. "Can you imagine doing this a century ago? The lightkeeper would have to carry a lantern—there was no electricity. Storms would be raging outside. I bet the ocean surrounded this place when conditions were right."

"It would take some bravery, that's for sure. That's not to mention the fact that there probably weren't many people even living here on the island. It would be isolated." Something about her words conveyed a deeper understanding.

She'd felt isolated since she arrived here, hadn't she? She'd had no one to open up to. No one she could share her troubles with.

Ty paced himself as they continued to climb. The ascent could be grueling to those not used to it, and there was no need to hurry.

"So I'm still trying to wrap my head around the fact that you're Cady Matthews." He purposefully turned the subject from Orion, sensing that Cassidy needed a reprieve from her thoughts.

"You really can—and should—call me Cassidy."

"I think I can handle that. But I'm trying to put together your background—your real one. Seattle detective. Crazy brave woman who went undercover with one of the world's most dangerous gangs. Tell me more."

"My dad is Max Matthews," she said.

Ty paused for a step. "The tech genius, financial guru, and Alpha Tech founder and CEO?"

She nodded almost robotically. "He's the one."

"So . . . your father owns the company I just got the grant from?"

"That's right. But he has no idea you're associated with me. You got that grant on your own merit. In fact, my parents don't know where I am. I told them I was taking an extended vacation. It only took them six weeks to realize something was wrong."

Her statement said it all. Her parents were rich and powerful and . . . absent.

A pang of compassion shot through him. "I'm sorry,

Cass."

"It's okay. I think that's why your family amazes me so much. They're everything I always wanted when growing up."

"My parents adore you." He meant the words. His mom constantly asked about Cassidy and mentioned how she couldn't wait to see her again.

They took a few more steps, halfway up now.

"That means a lot." Cassidy paused for a breath before continuing. "My dad always pushed me to go further, do better. My best was never enough. I still carry a lot of that twisted thinking with me. That unreasonable push to go beyond myself in order to become a success."

Pieces—images—of her past played in Ty's mind. "I can only imagine. Were you raised by nannies?"

"You know it." Cassidy was silent a moment. "When you and I first met, Ty, I know I was hard on you. But the truth is that I've been around a lot of men who've acted like pigs. I . . . I think I mentioned before that I discovered my father was having an affair when I was only thirteen."

"I can't even imagine."

"Dad told me not to tell Mom, that the news would destroy her, and it would be my fault. I believed him." She rubbed her throat, as if it were sore. "Later I found out it wasn't the first . . . or the last. I guess that should explain why I had a bit of distrust in you. Or men in general. The one man I looked up to . . ."

She didn't finish. She didn't need to.

Ty paused right there on the stairway and pulled her close. "I'm not that guy, Cassidy."

She nodded, but the motion looked strained—no doubt, but still with emotional baggage. "I know."

The huskiness in her voice made it clear she believed him—a fact that thrilled him.

"I feel like we have a lot of catching up to do." Almost like he had to get to know her all over again.

"We do." A touch of uncertainty wavered in her voice. "And I hope we'll have plenty of time for that later."

They reached the top and stepped out, the breeze nearly knocking them over. "Just watch that railing right there." Ty pointed to a suspect area. "We're securing it, but it's a little more complicated than simply nailing it back in place."

"I think I'll stay far away." Cassidy's gaze spanned the ocean that stretched infinitely before them. "It's really magnificent up here, Ty."

He wrapped his arms around her and stared out with her. "It is, isn't it? I've been wanting to show you this for a while. I never imagined today's events would lead to it."

Silence stretched, and Ty gave Cassidy the space she needed.

Maybe he needed some as well.

Because he'd fallen in love with the daughter of one of the wealthiest men in the country. With a detective who'd angered one of the most dangerous gangs around. That was a lot to process.

In truth—in his experience, at least—people seemed to naturally want to return to their roots.

Cassidy had a life back in Seattle. An established one. An established career. She didn't want or need for anything.

Ty would be foolish to think she'd be happy staying here at Lantern Beach, maybe settling down one day in a little cottage. Her mom probably had closets bigger than his place.

That didn't mean that Cassidy wasn't different. But the chances of her truly being content immersed in island life seemed to be slipping away faster than sand through his hands. He'd be a fool if he didn't acknowledge that reality, acknowledge the truth that things would change between them.

He stared out over the horizon—a large expanse that could make the most important person realize his or her place. Right now, he saw a trawler in the distance with seagulls flocking around it trying to steal today's catch. The ferry that shuttled people back and forth between islands also moved across the water. Everything looked so normal—yet nothing was the same.

Suddenly, Cassidy tensed in his arms.

"Ty, did you see that?" she asked.

He followed her gaze. As clear as day, a man emerged from the maritime forest surrounding the north side of the lighthouse. Kujo *had* been barking at something.

Ty had to get Cassidy out of sight. Now.

CASSIDY FLEW DOWN THE STAIRCASE. She wasn't sure who was pulling whom. She and Ty were both anxious to get out of sight and to figure out who'd been in those woods.

Someone lurking in the woods usually equaled one thing: trouble.

"You should stay here," Ty said when they reached the base of the stairs.

"I'm not sending you out there alone."

Ty hesitated, his breathing heavy. He wanted to argue. She could see it in his eyes. But instead he nodded. "Fine."

In record time, they made it through the quarters and to the door. They darted outside, Kujo on their heels. In the distance, Cassidy saw a man dressed in black moving along the edge of the tree line.

Ty pulled the gun from his waistband and paused. "Cassidy?"

"Yes?" The sun beat down on her, causing sweat to appear, only to be swept away seconds later by the breeze.

"I know you're a detective and you're used to being in charge," he said. "But wait here behind my truck for a moment. Please."

"But—"

"Please, Cassidy."

She bit back her arguments and conceded. "Okay. But don't get yourself killed."

She watched from behind his truck, waiting anxiously to see what would happen.

Her heart pounded in her ears with anticipation. Fear.

"Step out." Ty moved closer to the woods, ducking behind an old brick entryway to the lighthouse. "With your hands up."

Cassidy stayed behind the truck but moved closer, anxious to see what would happen. Praying that Ty wouldn't be harmed.

Her breath caught when someone emerged from the foliage.

"It's me." The man lifted his hands. "Don't shoot."

The air left Cassidy's lungs in a whoosh. Jimmy James? What in the world was going on?

Ty lowered his gun but remained on edge as he moved closer to his friend. Cassidy followed behind, anxious to hear the man's excuse.

Jimmy James was a large man—big and burly, like

Popeye on steroids. He looked tough, not only because of his large muscles but because of his rough demeanor —a missing tooth, tattoos, the general grimace he sported.

Upon closer inspection, Cassidy noted he wasn't actually wearing black. Instead, it was navy-blue jean shorts and a dark T-shirt.

"I'm sorry, man," Jimmy James said, his hands still in the air.

"What are you doing here, Jimmy James?" The irritation in Ty's voice was unmistakable.

The man raised his chin in defiance. "I was supposed to meet someone out here."

"In the woods? What's so secretive?" Ty asked.

Jimmy James shrugged. "Nothing. Just some business I have going on the side."

Ty shifted, his eyes narrowed with frustration. "You know I consider you a friend. But you're going to have to explain more than that."

The dockworker remained frozen a moment, as if considering his options. Finally, he let out a sigh. "I don't know. I don't want any trouble."

"Then explain before I call the police."

"This isn't your property either, you know." He raised his chin again.

"But I am here with permission," Ty said. "Are you?"

"Lots of people come out here to gawk." Some of his stubbornness began to shrink ever-so-slightly, but his argument sounded weak, at best. Certainly he was realizing that.

"Jimmy James . . ." Warning strained Ty's voice.

"Okay, okay." He fidgeted again before letting out a defeated sigh. "I was going to meet someone out here. They were buying some . . . some . . ."

Cassidy waited, holding her breath as she prepared herself for what he had to say.

He shrugged, almost looking embarrassed. That was it. He was *embarrassed*, she realized. His cheeks were even turning red.

"Some purses, okay." He folded his meaty arms across his expansive chest. "I was going to sell some purses."

"What?" Ty said.

His voice echoed the surprise Cassidy felt. That wasn't what she'd been expecting to hear. Drugs? Maybe. Weapons? Another possibility. But not handbags.

"They're knockoffs," Jimmy James muttered. "I'm just the go-between for a seller and his buyers. It makes enough for me to buy groceries. Since I work at the docks, I'm in a good position to do the job."

"How long have you been doing this?" Cassidy asked, feeling both relieved and let down. Part of her had hoped for answers. But at least there was no danger here. Not for the moment anyway.

"Three years."

"Wow. That long." Ty shook his head, disbelief in his

voice. "And why here? If you give some boxes to someone, who's going to know what's inside?"

"It's complicated."

"You might be surprised what we understand," Ty said. "And where are these so-called purses?"

"I pick them up here. When I see the boat coming, I go over to meet it. This guy doesn't want anyone to see his face. Then I distribute the goods at the docks."

"Interesting," Ty said.

"Lots of illegal stuff goes down here at the Point," Jimmy James said. "It's secluded. No one wants to venture out here at night alone. It's the perfect spot for trouble. Speaking of, what are you two doing here?"

Ty's jaw hardened. "I was showing Cassidy the lighthouse."

"Do you always get so defensive when someone else shows up at a location where you're not supposed to be?"

So Jimmy James was more observant than Cassidy had given him credit for. He'd seemed like a meathead, for lack of a better term. He had a history with drugs, and using them was known to kill off brain cells.

"There have been some strange things going on around town lately," Cassidy said. "You can never be too careful."

Jimmy James's gaze fell on her. "Speaking of strange things, someone was asking about you yesterday."

Her spine stiffened. "Is that right? Who was it?"

"I don't know." He shrugged. "It was at night. I couldn't see him."

"What did he ask?" Ty stepped closer, the warrior inside him surfacing in his intimidating stance.

"About some lady here in town who'd helped break up a human-trafficking ring."

Cassidy sucked in a breath. Someone was looking for her—*she* was that person. A month ago, she'd helped three women who escaped from captivity. Their faces appeared in Cassidy's mind, and she wondered about them. Wondered how they were doing.

"What did you tell him?"

"I asked him why he wanted to know."

"And he said?" Ty asked.

"Claimed he was a reporter," Jimmy James said. "But I didn't believe him. He seemed shifty."

"Could you identify this man?" Cassidy's heart raced as if on the verge of crossing the first of many finish lines.

"Sorry. I can't. White guy. Maybe in his thirties. I don't think he wanted me to see his face."

Ty and Cassidy exchanged a glance. It wasn't much. Hardly anything, for that matter. Too many people in town fit that vague description.

Finally, Ty clarified, "And you didn't admit that you knew Cassidy?"

"Nah, man. I didn't think it was any of his business. If he was a reporter, he could do his own homework."

"If he comes back, will you let us know?" Ty asked.

"Sure thing." Jimmy James leveled his gaze. "As long as you keep quiet about my purse operation."

———

Ty and Cassidy went back into the lighthouse after talking to Jimmy James. From the window, Cassidy watched the scene outside. Sure enough, a boat pulled up and Jimmy James grabbed some boxes from inside.

Selling knockoff purses was illegal—a violation of trademark. The whole thing seemed strange. Yet she had bigger issues to deal with at the moment. Like staying alive.

"Purses?" Cassidy started, glancing back at Ty.

Ty glared at the scene outside, looking more irritated than anything else.

"Nothing surprises me anymore. And purses aren't what concern me most," Ty said. "What does bother me is the man asking about you at the docks. Orion?"

Cassidy paced away from the window, attempting to gather her thoughts. "I'm trying to step outside myself for a second here . . . Orion seems like a natural choice. But I also know my parents hired a PI. I asked Samuel—he's my contact—to get them to call the man off. I don't know if it worked or not."

Ty lowered himself on the couch, leaning forward in thought. "So it could be this PI?"

"It's a possibility," Cassidy said.

"I suppose it's also possible that this *is* connected with that human-trafficking ring."

"The likelihood that two different sets of criminals are looking for me is unlikely."

She couldn't believe those words were even leaving her mouth. They seemed absurd, but close enough to the edge of reality to frighten her.

"You've made yourself a target," Ty said. "All in the name of justice, but a target none-the-less."

"I can't argue that."

Ty shifted again and turned toward her. "Did you think any more about involving Mac?"

She released a pent-up breath, still wrestling with what the right answer was. The lines felt so blurry sometimes. But Mac was a friend . . . and she could use his help.

"Let's talk to him," Cassidy said. "But don't share details. We'll tell him that I'm in trouble, and we need his assistance. Okay?"

"I'll call him right now. I'm sure he'll do whatever he can to help."

While Ty made his phone call, Cassidy stepped into the kitchen, which currently consisted of some unfinished lower cabinets and a rusty sink. She had to talk to Samuel. He needed to know what was happening.

She dug out her hidden cell phone, the one used only for emergencies, and dialed his number. He answered on the first ring.

"What's going on, Cassidy?" His deep voice sounded across the line.

She didn't waste any time with small talk and jumped right to the point. "I think I saw Orion, Samuel."

Silence stretched for a minute. "You need to leave. Now."

Cassidy had known that's what he would say, and she braced herself for the progression of this conversation. It wasn't going to go well. "I'm staying, Samuel."

"Why would you do that? You know what he'll do if he finds you. Do I need to remind you what happened to other women? The ones DH-7 believed were you?"

Cassidy shuddered. No, he didn't need to remind her. The images were burned into her mind. Those women—the ones who'd been mistaken for Cassidy—hadn't died pleasant deaths. Their final moments had been long and torturous—the definition of suffering.

"I know, Samuel. But I want to confirm it *is* Orion first."

"Don't take the chance."

"He'll just keep finding me. You and I both know it's true." Her voice cracked with emotion. But he couldn't deny the honesty of her words. This was a chase that would never end.

"We need you at this trial, Cassidy."

"I know." Again, the reminder that what Cassidy could offer was more important than who she was struck her like a slap in the face.

Samuel finally sighed. "I don't like this. If you're not leaving then I want daily updates so I know you're alive."

"I can do that." She paused, one question lingering in her head above the rest. She almost didn't want to ask. "How did he find me, Samuel?"

"I have no idea. I haven't told a soul. As far as I know, only you and I know."

Ryan Samson's image came to mind. He was the only other person who knew she was leaving—but not where she was going.

At the thought of him, Cassidy shifted. She'd thought she was going to marry the man at one time, and then he'd disappeared from her life, like Cassidy had never even existed. When she'd met Ty, she realized just how much her relationship with Ryan had lacked. She didn't regret ending that relationship one bit.

She also remembered they suspected someone on the inside. It was the only way that safe house had been compromised. Who was the mole? Had Ryan opened up to the wrong person about what was going on? Had someone working with Samuel gone through his files?

Cassidy had no idea. And being thousands of miles away, she had no way of researching it further.

"Be safe, Cassidy," Samuel said. "There's a lot riding on your testimony."

"I know, and I will be."

Just as she hung up with Samuel, her phone rang— her other cell phone. It was Serena. Something told her it was imperative she answer.

"Serena, what's going on?" she asked.

"I just got to your place to pick up Elsa," she started.

Cassidy had forgotten to tell her not to come today. With everything going on, the detail had slipped her mind. "Okay . . ."

"Something seemed different about your house, so I went on the deck," Serena said. "Cassidy, it looks like someone broke into your place. One of the windows above your door was smashed."

Cassidy's heart pounded in her ears. All signs were pointing to the confirmation that Orion had found her.

CHAPTER
SIX

AS SOON AS Ty came back into the room, Cassidy gave him the update from Serena.

"I don't like this." Ty frowned, and it was obvious that reality was setting in. The situation was a lot for anyone to digest.

"I don't either. But I need to know if Orion is behind all this."

Surprise registered across his face. "How exactly do you propose to figure that out?"

Cassidy took a deep breath before saying, "I'm not going to wait for him to find me, Ty. I need to root him out."

"Are you sure that's a good idea? I mean, I don't want you to run. But I don't relish the idea of you searching for him either."

"You said I should stand my ground. I can't just sit here and do nothing, biding my time until he makes his move." She didn't like feeling helpless or that Orion was the one calling the shots. No, that wasn't how she operated. Not in Seattle and not in Lantern Beach.

Ty's face tightened. "I don't like this. Have I mentioned that?"

"Multiple times."

He let out a sigh and ran a hand over his face. "Keep wearing that baseball cap and the sunglasses. Even if Orion sees you, he won't recognize you at first. I mean, I'm basing that purely on the cartoons of Commotio Cordis that were created from your past likeness."

"I look nothing like Japanese anime in my current form." Cassidy flashed a smile, trying to add some humor to the tense situation for both her sake and Ty's. But it didn't work. Ty remained tense.

"You shouldn't go anywhere without me," Ty said. "Not to sound like a misogynist. But there is safety in numbers."

"Once again, I agree."

"It's going to be difficult to find him, especially since it's tourist season. I'd guess, from what you told me, that he's not the type to rent a house. There's usually a lot of paperwork and planning involved with that. Which leaves the inn and the campground. I say we start there."

Finally, Cassidy nodded. She liked hearing Ty's thought process, hearing him use his experience in the real world. He sounded so knowledgeable and sure of himself—two things that were very attractive.

"Okay then," she said. "Let's do it."

Ten minutes later, they were heading down the road. They dropped Kujo off at Austin's. Meanwhile, Mac was going to look into the break-in at Cassidy's place. It was better if Cassidy stayed away until they had more information. Cassidy told Serena to take a day off from selling ice cream while they gathered their thoughts more.

Cassidy stole a glance at Ty as they drove, noting the tight set of his jaw and the determination in his gaze. But there was something more, wasn't there? Was it a hint of sadness or melancholy? She wasn't sure, and this wasn't the time to ask.

Instead, she lifted up thanks that he was beside her now.

If she ever got married, she'd always wanted it to be to someone who'd be her partner, her equal—someone who shared mutual respect with her. Everything on her list had been checked off with Ty—checked off ten times over.

They pulled up to the one and only inn in town. It was an old plantation-style building with white shingles and a double balcony, located on the water. However, the elements hadn't been kind to the place. Its fixtures appeared rusty, the paint was peeling, several shingles were missing, and the septic tank was partially exposed.

Ty stared at it a long moment before turning toward her. "Do you want to wait here while I go inside?"

"Not a chance." This was her fight, and she wasn't

going to let anyone drown while trying to save her. Not if she had anything to do about it.

"If Orion is a guest here, he could see you."

She tugged down her hat and slid on her sunglasses. She acknowledged the truth in his words. She'd thought it through, and it was a chance she was willing to take. "I'll be careful."

"Okay then. Let's go."

They climbed the wooden steps to the building and stepped into the foyer. A woman behind the desk smiled at them pensively. She had a tight bun, librarian-like glasses, and wore a dowdy white shirt.

"We're all full," she announced, barely glancing up from the novel she was reading. "I'm sorry."

"We don't need a room." Ty paused in front of the registration desk, his figure imposing in the dainty space. "We're actually looking for someone who might be staying here."

"I can't give out personal information on our guests." Her face tightened with stubbornness and a hint of suspicion.

"Can I be honest with you?" Cassidy leaned closer, her fingers skimming the glossy wood countertop beneath them. Polish moistened her skin—lemon scented polish that would probably follow her the rest of the day. Cassidy kept her voice low. Reasoning wouldn't work, so she'd appeal to the woman's emotions instead.

"Please do."

"I own Elsa, the ice cream truck."

The woman raised her chin and offered a half-shrug. "I know. The haunted ice cream truck is a legend around here. I heard people came into town just to see it."

This was the first Cassidy had heard about it. But that wasn't important right now.

"Someone bought something from me." Cassidy paused. "Well, *bought* isn't the right word. He *said* he was going to buy something, but then he took off without paying. I heard he was staying here."

The woman's eyes widened, and suddenly Cassidy had her full attention. "For real? There might be a criminal staying here?"

Cassidy nodded. "I know it's only ice cream, and it doesn't seem like a big deal. But if someone steals something as small as ice cream, then there's a chance they'll stiff you too. It's like one of my friends used to say—integrity starts with the small stuff."

Day-at-a-Glance, 01-01.

"You might be right." The woman still looked pensive and uncertain. Maybe even a touch frightened now.

Cassidy waited for it to play out, giving the woman time to wrestle with her thoughts. But she couldn't give her enough time to overthink it either.

The clerk put her book down and rolled her shoulders back. "What does this guy look like?"

A brief flash of relief rushed through Cassidy. Maybe she was getting somewhere. Maybe.

"He's probably six three," Cassidy said. "He had

some pretty huge muscles. Dark hair that's longer on top."

The woman thought about it a moment before shaking her head. "I'm sorry. I wish I could help, but I haven't seen anyone matching that description."

"I see." Cassidy leaned close again. "Do me a favor? If he does show up, please don't mention you've seen me. I want to catch him by surprise."

"I won't. For what it's worth, I hope you find him. Stealing is stealing."

"I agree," Cassidy said. "And thanks again."

Well, at least that answered one question—Orion wasn't staying here. But Cassidy's job was far from over.

Cassidy and Ty stepped outside and back into the August heat. Sweltering seemed like an understatement for its intensity, and there wasn't a cloud in sight. Nope, this heat would be with them for the rest of the day.

Ty took her elbow as they crossed the gravel parking lot. "Is that your cover story?"

"It worked. Here, at least."

"What about Lisa, Austin, and the gang? Could we let them know *something* is going on without letting them know *what's* going on?"

Cassidy cringed. Lying to people she considered her friends was complicated and left her uneasy. Yet what other choice did she have? "I hate to lie to them. But . . ."

"We need to extend your cover. That is the only thing that makes sense, at this point."

Cassidy nodded, grateful Ty understood her point of view. "Then yes. If you're comfortable with it, let's proceed. But not with the ice cream theft story. They'll see through that. I have another idea. First, let's hit the campground."

CHAPTER
SEVEN

BEFORE THEY LEFT the parking lot, Ty's phone rang. It was Mac, so Ty put him on speaker.

"Hey, Chief," Ty said. "What's going on? Cassidy's listening."

"Perfect. I'm at Cassidy's place now," Mac said. "Someone's definitely been here and rifled through things. The TV is gone, as well as the computer."

"What?" Cassidy said. "What sense does that make?"

Why would Orion take those things? Unless it was to throw everyone off and cover his tracks. It was the only logical conclusion.

"I just happened to talk to Bozoman." Bozoman was what Mac called the current police chief, Alan Bozeman. The name, unfortunately, was all too appropriate. "I casually asked about any recent crimes in the area—not mentioning the one at your house. It turns out there's been a rash of robberies in this area over the past two weeks."

"Really?" Cassidy said. Again, was this something disconnected? It seemed so unlikely. But maybe it was a possibility. She didn't want to be closed-minded.

"Really," Mac said. "I heard a little about it on the police scanner, but I wanted to confirm. It's mostly petty thefts—TVs and electronics. Probably some kids selling the stuff for drug money. Seen it before."

"Thanks for your help," Cassidy said.

"Anytime. Oh, and I nailed a board up over your broken window until someone can come fix it."

"I appreciate that."

"I'll keep my ears open for more information on the break-ins. Send me a picture of that guy who's giving you trouble, and I'll keep my eyes open for him too."

"Thanks, Mac." Cassidy smiled. "I appreciate that."

After Ty hung up, they remained in the parking lot. Biting flies dived at the windows, making Cassidy glad the AC was on. Those things were vicious.

Kind of like life could be sometimes.

She leaned her head back against the seat, fighting feelings of being overwhelmed. Her thoughts just kept circling and circling, as if they had no place to land.

"This keeps getting stranger and stranger," Cassidy finally said.

"You can say that again."

"Whoever did this, broke in during the middle of the day," Cassidy said, still trying to fit the pieces together. "Why would they do that? It's risky."

"Maybe they know most people are at the beach and figure it's a good time to strike. Thieves are always breaking into cars at the beach. Tourists often leave them unlocked with their valuables inside. Vacationers think the area is safe—and it generally is—but there are people who prey on others, and they live off those assumptions."

"Maybe you're right." But Cassidy still wasn't convinced. She had to keep searching for answers. "I say we go check out the campground now. Maybe Orion is staying there. I just know I can't sit around not doing anything."

"Let's go."

———

Ty and Cassidy had talked to several people at the campground, but no one had seen Orion. It was another dead-end. Maybe the man really had rented a house for the week. Occasionally, deals popped up at the last minute, or there were even some people who rented out rooms in their homes through online websites.

Lines of worry had formed on Cassidy's face. This was taking a toll on her, and the fight was just starting. She'd already been through so much. The thought of her walking through this by herself made Ty's heart hurt for her. No one should have to carry that kind of burden alone.

"How about we visit Lisa?" Ty suggested. "She's a

good contact for this. A lot of people come into her restaurant."

Cassidy nodded, still seeming like a mix of dread and fire collided inside her, making her gaze uneasy. "Okay, let's do it."

Ty slipped his hands into hers, wishing he could say something to make all of this better. But there was nothing he could say that would do that. He'd just be there for her.

She was quiet on the ride to the Crazy Chefette, and he gave her time with her thoughts. He needed some with his own thoughts, for that matter.

Lisa greeted them at the door with a big grin on her face and her lab coat splattered with remnants of some new creation. A scientist-turned-chef, she loved playing with crazy food combinations. The lithe blonde's eyes always danced with creativity and a touch of unhinged brilliance.

"Fancy seeing you two here," she said. "I thought you'd be out selling ice cream. People would pay an arm and leg for a cool refreshment on a day like today."

"Long story," Cassidy said. "And are you acting as hostess today or were you waiting for us?"

"Someone called in sick so I'm running around like a chicken with her head cut off. Hey, that should be the name of one of my new dishes." She looked off into the distance, her brain already hard at work. "Anyway, let me get you seats. You want to sit with Austin and Skye? They're here."

Cassidy glanced at Ty and nodded. "Yeah, that sounds great."

They took a seat beside their friends. Before they could strike up any type of conversation, Lisa continued talking.

"Ashley, bring out my experiment," she called to one of her waitresses. "I was hoping everyone would be here to act as my lab rats . . . I mean, taste testers."

Lisa and her experiments sure did make life interesting. People never knew what her mad scientist persona would dream up.

A moment later, a waitress appeared with some cupcakes.

"These are on the house," Lisa said with a wide grin.

Ty stared at the chocolate cupcakes with orange icing, wondering what was wrong with them. Little orange sprinkles of some sort graced the top.

"What are these?" Austin leaned closer to examine them, looking like he'd come straight from a construction site, with his black T-shirt, jeans, and a baseball cap he wore backwards.

"I thought you'd never ask." Lisa clapped. "Cheetos cupcakes."

Ty cringed at the thought of eating Cheetos-flavored sweets. As he glanced around the table, everyone seemed to share the sentiment.

"They're delicious," Lisa said. "I promise."

"I'll save mine for dessert," Cassidy said.

"Yeah, me too," Skye said.

"Makes the most sense," Austin agreed.

Cassidy shifted, her momentary humor disappearing. "Hey, Lisa. Before you go, can I talk to you? All of you."

Lisa's expression turned from giddy to serious. "Sure thing."

"What's going on?" Austin asked. "Does this have something to do with you dropping off Kujo earlier?"

"Kind of. I need to tell you all something." Cassidy glanced around the table.

Ty put a hand on her back, encouraging her to continue.

"There's a man in town looking for me," she started. "We have a history. A very bad one. And I'm afraid of what he'll do if he finds me."

Skye gasped softly. "Like a boyfriend?"

Cassidy shrugged, that one action indicating there was more to the story than she wanted to share. "Something like that. Anyway, it's extremely important that if you see him or if he asks you about me, that you tell him I'm not here. I'm out of town. I hate to ask you to lie. But, it's like I said, if he finds me—"

"He'll hurt you." Austin's face hardened. "We're not going to let that happen. What does this guy look like?"

Cassidy pulled out her phone and found his picture. "This isn't the best picture of him. He appears to have cleaned up his act before coming here."

They passed the phone around, each staring at the picture. Skye squinted when she saw the photo. "I just can't see you being with someone like that."

Cassidy shrugged. "I guess we all have secrets and regrets from our past."

"Yes, we do," Skye agreed.

"You've seen him in town?" Lisa asked, her gaze bouncing from the phone back to Cassidy.

"This morning," Cassidy said.

"So what are you going to do?" Austin asked. "Are you leaving?"

"No, I've decided to stand my ground," Cassidy said. "For better or worse. I can't run every time he finds me. I need to claim my life again."

"I'm proud of you," Lisa said. "That's not an easy choice to make."

Something about the way she said the words made Ty wonder if there was more to Lisa's story than she'd shared in Bible study.

"You just want us to tell him you're not here?" Austin asked. "Or you want us to run him out of town?"

Cassidy swung her head back and forth. "I can't have you getting hurt because of me. I'd never forgive myself if something happened to one of you because of this. Just tell him you don't recognize me."

"We can think of ways to make his stay here very unpleasant," Skye said. "I can add some Visine to his water. Or throw some rotting fruit outside the place where he's staying. Or maybe something with fire ants."

"Fire ants?" Austin asked.

Skye shrugged. "Long story."

"We think he could be staying at the campground where you are," Ty said. "We don't know that for sure."

"I'll keep my eyes open," Skye said.

Skye lived there because housing in the area was so expensive. It wasn't unheard of for locals to park an RV at the campground and settle there permanently.

"And I'll watch for him here at the Crazy Chefette as well," Lisa said. "You're one of us now, Cassidy. We look out for one another."

Cassidy smiled. Maybe the first smile since she'd revealed her past to Ty.

"Now, how about some food?" Lisa asked. "I'd hate for those Cheetos cupcakes to go to waste!"

Thirty minutes later, they were back in Ty's truck and headed down the road again.

He drove a restored antique Chevy pickup that turned heads wherever they went. The vehicle was beautiful, and every detail had been done with attention and precision. There was nothing like taking a ride in it on temperate nights with the windows down and classic music from the fifties blaring from the speakers.

Cassidy's thoughts turned over in her mind as she rode. Her new group of friends here were amazing. Just hearing that they thought of her as one of the gang meant the world to her. Not to mention that Lisa kept her well-fed. The Cheetos cupcake hadn't been that bad.

She glanced over at Ty and sensed a heaviness about

him. Since she'd revealed so many of her secrets, she didn't want to push him to talk. When it was time, he would.

Besides, she was preoccupied with her own thoughts.

They shifted from her new friends to Orion. She reviewed the facts she had against the questions that remained. First, Cassidy had thought she'd seen him. Then she'd learned a man had asked about her at the docks. Lastly, her house had been broken into.

Nothing definitive. In fact, she could justify each as a fluke because, in a court of law, none of it would hold up.

Yet she couldn't ignore it either.

Her dad had told her that sometimes the mind tried too hard to make sense of things. It was why people saw images in clouds and hearts in puddles. It was why a person attempted to order events and believe there was a purpose in their sequences.

"Thanks for being here, Ty." Cassidy's voice came out husky with emotion.

"Of course. Thank you for trusting me with your secret."

Silence stretched for a moment as they cruised down the street, dodging tourists who hurried across the road loaded down with inner tubes and beach chairs and wagons with puffy wheels made for traveling on the sand.

Ty pressed on the brakes to slow the pickup.

But nothing happened.

A surge of adrenaline raced through Cassidy's blood. "What's wrong?"

"It's my brakes. They've gone out." He lay on his horn.

Tourists scrambled from the road, some shouting and raising their hands in anger at him.

Irate beachgoers were the least of their worries right now.

They still had to pass through the downtown area without harming anyone—or themselves.

"Hold on, Cassidy," Ty muttered. "I'm not sure how this is going to end."

CHAPTER
EIGHT

CASSIDY GRIPPED the armrest as they coasted down the road.

Please, Lord, protect the people around us.

Another car, heading toward the intersection they approached, braked suddenly and honked at them.

"Sorry," Ty muttered, though the driver couldn't hear him.

He pumped the brakes again. His other foot was off the accelerator, but they weren't slowing down nearly fast enough. There were too many people in this area—people who expected the right-of-way belonged to pedestrians.

Ty pounded his horn again, warning people to get out of the way. People jumped back from the road, throwing more dirty looks and disgruntled words his way.

"We need to head toward the lighthouse," he said.

"That road is usually empty, and the area around the road is sandy. That will definitely make us stop."

"We just have to get through town without harming anyone first." Cassidy squeezed the armrest again.

"That's the key," Ty said through clenched teeth.

Finally, they hit the end of town, the truck still coasting. At the first area where the sand created deep canyons beside the road, Ty jerked the wheel. The truck lurched from the asphalt and bounced onto the soft sand.

They lurched as all four wheels left the thick pavement. Finally, the truck rolled to a stop.

Neither spoke for a minute. Cassidy's heart pounded in her chest as her thoughts caught up with her adrenaline.

"That was close," she said.

"Are you okay?" Ty turned toward her, concern in his gaze.

She nodded. "Yeah, you?"

"I'm fine. I've got to check this out." He hopped from the truck.

Cassidy followed, anxious to see for herself what had happened. "What do you think? Was the brake line cut?"

She didn't want to ask, but she had to know. She kept the second part of her question silent, though. The question that asked, Had Orion done this?

Ty lay on his back and pulled himself beneath the truck. "It doesn't appear to be tampered with. I can't say for sure what happened. It is an old truck. Things happen sometimes."

Cassidy drew her lips into a tight line. Yes, things did happen. But with Orion in town, she wasn't letting anything slide.

Speaking of Orion . . . she glanced at the nearby woods, watching for a sign of anything suspicious. A squirrel scampered from branch to branch. Some birds took a bath in one of the puddles between the trees. The wind rustled leaves.

But she didn't see anyone.

That didn't mean no one was out there, though.

Ty inched out from beneath the truck and leaned on his elbows. "I'm going to have to get a tow out of this sand. Austin should be able to do that with his truck. Until then, let's walk back to the lighthouse."

"Sounds good."

They started side by side, Ty slipping an arm around her back. "You sure you're okay?"

"Yeah, just . . . I don't even know how to describe how I'm feeling right now. Just preoccupied, I suppose."

"Hopefully we'll get some answers soon."

Just then, her secret cell phone rang. It had to be Samuel calling.

"Speaking of which . . ." she muttered. "Excuse me a minute."

She put the phone to her ear, turning away from the wind so she could hear better. "What's going on?"

"I talked to our other agent who's undercover with

DH-7," Samuel started. "He heard Orion is looking for you. The last update he got was that Orion was in South Carolina or Georgia. Somewhere in that general vicinity."

"That doesn't mean he's not here."

"No, it doesn't. But I wanted to let you know. Any updates on your end?"

Cassidy scanned the area again. Just trees and sand and the tip of the lighthouse down the road peeking above it all. Yet it wasn't that simple. Danger could lurk anywhere. "No, not yet."

"Are you sure you don't want to leave, Cassidy?"

"I'd rather have my enemy within my sights than to run and not know if he's behind me."

"I can respect that. Be careful."

"Always." But as she hung up, her unsettled stomach churned.

———

At the lighthouse, Cassidy felt a moment of restlessness. Their vehicle was now stuck in the sand, which meant they were stuck here until someone towed the truck out. There was too much at stake to sit around and do nothing.

Ty approached her from behind and placed his hands on her arms. "You look like you're beside yourself."

"I guess I am. I just want answers."

"How about we go for a walk?" Ty said. "We know

no one followed us, and fresh air will do you good. We have a good half an hour until Austin arrives. I just called him."

She thought about it a moment before nodding. "Okay then. We just need to keep our eyes open. And bring guns."

"Never leave home without one."

"I knew I liked you for some reason." Cassidy smiled, for a few seconds feeling like this craziness didn't exist. As quickly as the lightheartedness appeared, it was gone.

He took her hand, and they walked outside, toward the roaring ocean. It crashed against the rock jetty built decades ago to protect the lighthouse. Apparently, the ocean had shifted and deposited more sand around the structure, securing its place here on the island in recent years.

That was if the few bits of history Cassidy had learned were accurate.

They walked away from the ocean, toward the inlet that cut around the island, merging the sound waters into the salty Atlantic.

Cassidy paused and pointed to something down the beach. "Please don't tell me another boat washed ashore."

Last time she'd found one, she'd nearly blown her cover trying to figure out how it had gotten spit out by the ocean right in front of her home. Again, images of the women aboard the craft filled her mind. How was Rose doing? Stubborn, rebellious, rough-around-the-edges Rose? Or the always frightened Kat. Or Trina, who'd been neglected and abandoned for most of her life.

"That's the *August Moon*," Ty said. "She's been there for three years now."

"Really? I didn't even see her from the lighthouse earlier."

"That's because these trees are perfectly placed and conceal it."

"Nice."

Ty nodded. "The story is that a wealthy businessman from up north was having her towed from Florida when a storm came up. The boat broke free and came ashore. The guys the boat's owner hired stayed with the vessel for the first month. Locals even brought them food. Eventually, the owner realized it was going to cost more to fix the situation than it was worth, so he cut his losses and left it here."

"Interesting." They got closer, and Cassidy examined the boat more thoroughly. Local kids had apparently sprayed graffiti on the backside of the vessel, making it more a piece of artwork than a piece of wreckage. The other side was still weathered and brown.

"These waters have been dangerous for centuries," Ty said. "There's a reason it's considered part of the Graveyard of the Atlantic.

"So when I say there's danger surrounding this island, I'm not exaggerating."

Ty shook his head. "In more than one way."

Cassidy shivered and stared out over the water. "How can something so beautiful hold such a threat?"

Ty shrugged, his gaze clouding for a minute, as if he were being transported back in time. "Isn't that life? You know, most of the terrorists I fought started with good intentions. I know that sounds crazy. But they started with an ideal that got blown up into something irrational. They started by fighting for what they believed in—and that can be a beautiful thing. But that passion and those ideals can turn ugly. I guess that's the way life works. The line between good and evil, beauty and ugliness, danger and safety—it's thin."

"You're right." Cassidy sat beside the *August Moon* and leaned against the boat's hull. Ty sat beside her, but at an angle so he could keep an eye out for trouble.

Cassidy watched the waves a minute. The currents here clashed together, one from the north and the other from the south. She shuddered to think about someone who wasn't a strong swimmer getting caught in the tumultuous waters.

Emotionally, she could relate. She felt like that swimmer with danger coming at her from multiple sides. She had to be careful, or the person who ventured out to rescue her would get caught in the currents as well.

After a few minutes of silence, Cassidy asked, "How's your mom?"

Cassidy had gotten some texts from Del since the woman's cancer came back and she'd begun treatments.

But they hadn't actually talked lately even though Cassidy thought about her often.

Ty stared out over the water, the wind ruffling his already messy hair and the sun's harsh angle emphasizing his pensive expression. "I guess this is a tough week of chemo. They've warned her that she'll start to lose her hair and nausea will set in with this treatment."

Compassion gripped her. Cancer was such a horrible disease, and fighting it could take so much out of a person. "I'm so sorry, Ty. I wish there was something I could do. I guess I'm learning that there are a lot of things out of my control."

"Mom's tough, and she's keeping a positive attitude. That goes a long way." He paused. "But I hate that she's having to go through this."

"Your mom is one of the strongest, most joyful women I've ever met." Del had welcomed Cassidy with open arms and taught her so much in the brief three days Ty's parents had been in town.

"She is." Ty paused. "Tell me more about your life, Cassidy. Your real life. Back in Seattle. I feel like there's so much I don't know about you. You told me a little earlier. I want to hear more."

She ran some sand through her fingers, her thoughts as tumultuous as the sea and as broken as the bits of shells shattered by the ocean. "What would you like to know?"

"Why'd you become a cop?" He picked up a broken whelk shell and tossed it absently in the water.

She let out a sigh as she remembered the events

leading up to the decision. She didn't talk about them often. In fact, she hadn't talked about that part of her past in months. "My best friend, Lucy, was murdered when she was seventeen. The police never found her killer. By then, I was already on the path of rebellion. I'd been offered softball scholarships, and I was pretty sure I was going to take one of those over getting a business degree and taking over my dad's company one day."

"I'm sure that didn't go over well." Ty glanced at her quickly before scanning the landscape behind them —mostly barren. Anyone would have a hard time sneaking up on them without giving themselves away.

"Not at all. I just had no interest in following in his footsteps, you know? I may be blood, but there are other people way more qualified. But after Lucy died, something lit inside me. I wanted to make a difference in people's lives—people whose worlds had been turned upside down by crime."

"Sounds noble. We've only got one chance when it comes to life on this earth. You don't want to look back one day with regrets."

Cassidy found a broken whelk also and tossed it. "I had to fight to find my way as a cop, not only against my parents, but because of the nature of the job. I know people think men and women are generally equal in this day and age, but that's not always reality. Police work is a male-dominated field."

"I can see that."

"Some people still think I became a detective only because of my dad." Cassidy paused. "I found out later he made a large donation to the police's nonprofit, which made me wonder if they were all correct. Maybe I did get the job because of him."

"That's got to be hard." Ty didn't sound like he felt sorry for her, only compassionate and understanding.

Cassidy was grateful for his listening ear, and it nudged her to open up more—something she rarely did. Something about the waves and the sand—and Ty —just put her spirit more at ease.

"The truth is that for my whole life I've never known if people liked me for me, or if they liked me because of what I could do for them." Her voice came out raspier than she wanted, but her words carried emotional weight. "It was easier to pour myself into my work. So that's what I did. I wanted to prove myself."

"It's easy to fall into that trap."

"I took the undercover assignment with DH-7, knowing it was risky and that I'd be putting my entire life on hold. But I was supposed to go in, get the information I needed, and then be done. I never anticipated killing the group's leader."

Now that she said the words aloud, new questions rammed into her mind. Why had she been picked for that assignment? She was a rich girl who worked the white-collar crime division. Yet she'd been singled out to go undercover with a street gang.

At the time, she'd thought she'd earned it on merit. But what if that wasn't the case at all? What if she'd been handpicked for a different reason?

The thought startled her. She'd have to examine that

line of questioning a little later.

"Then you came here to Lantern Beach?" Ty said.

"That's right. I'd never even heard of this place before, and I was terrified. But, back in Seattle, some men broke into the first safe house location and killed the guards. I knew it was a matter of time before they found me again if I stayed in Seattle. I was supposed to come here, bide my time, and then return for trial. But the date was pushed back . . . and I found myself liking it here . . . and I met you."

Ty squeezed her hand. "I'm grateful for that."

She glanced up at him, soaking in the contours of his face. The stubble that formed a shadow on his jaw and upper lip. His eyes that showed unyielding strength yet kindness too. "My old life seems far away, Ty, like something I don't want to go back to."

"But you have to." His words sounded dull.

"I have to go back for the trial. I just assumed I'd go back to being a detective. But . . . nothing seems certain right now."

"You've got me. That's certain."

His words filled her chest with warm goo. She reached up and kissed him quickly. "I'm so glad I've got you."

"Always."

Her cell phone buzzed, breaking the moment. It was Lisa.

"You'll never believe this, Cassidy," Lisa rushed. "Your ex came in an hour after you left. You've got to hear what he had to say."

CHAPTER
NINE

CASSIDY PUT the phone on speaker, her heart racing. She angled the phone against the breeze so Ty could hear also.

"Ty and I are both here," Cassidy said. "What did Orion say?"

"I don't know." Lisa's voice cracked with . . . something Cassidy couldn't identify. "It was weird, Cassidy. He . . . didn't give any indication that he was looking for you."

Cassidy's throat burned with emotions, with exclamations she wanted to shout out loud. She wanted to rebuke Lisa's words and insist she was mistaken.

She didn't, however. Instead, she asked, "What did he say?"

"He said his name was Rich and that he was from Missouri. He said he and his wife were married here, but she died in a car accident six months ago. This week would have been their three-year anniversary."

Cassidy's stomach lurched. That didn't make sense. He was obviously lying and trying to gain people's sympathy. Had Lisa really fallen for it? This was no time to say anything that might sound accusatory. Lisa was just a messenger.

"He sounds quite talkative," Cassidy said instead.

"He was. He . . . don't take this wrong, but he seemed pretty nice."

"Is that right?" Cassidy's gut twisted even tighter. She didn't like where this was going. Not one bit.

"Sorry. Maybe I shouldn't have said that." Apology stretched through Lisa's voice.

"No, I want the truth," Cassidy said. "Even if it's not what I want to hear."

When Cassidy shoved her emotions aside, she knew her words were honest. Gut reactions couldn't be trusted, and Cassidy was in so deep that she couldn't tell which end was up.

"Okay, good," Lisa said. "Because I feel a little bad saying it."

Cassidy swallowed hard, trying to keep herself in check.

"Is there anything else we should know?" Ty asked, seeming to sense how Cassidy wrestled with her thoughts.

"Well, I kept talking to him," Lisa said, the chatter from the restaurant creating a buzz through the phone line. "I tried to figure about where he was staying, but he didn't take the bait. I'm sorry. I wish I could have done more."

"No, you did a good job, Lisa," Cassidy said. "Thanks for letting me know."

"Anytime, Cassidy. I hope you get things figured out."

She hung up and turned toward Ty, waiting for his reaction, still uncertain how she felt. When Ty frowned, she prepared herself to hear something she wasn't going to like.

"Maybe we should face the possibility that he's not Orion," Ty said. "I know it's not what you want to hear. But we should be open-minded."

"I don't know." Cassidy's conflicting emotions were playing with her instincts, and she didn't like it. It was part of the reason she needed people around her who weren't blinded by fear or assumptions. "Either way, we expect the best, prepare for the worst."

Ty placed his hand on her back, the small act filling her with tremendous comfort. "I agree. We can't let down our guard. This is far from over, Cassidy. Something is going on. We'll figure out the truth eventually."

She shook her head, still working things through. Something wasn't fitting here. Either Cassidy was totally wrong, or she'd underestimated Orion. "Here's what's bugging me. The Orion I remember—he didn't seem like he'd be that good of an actor."

"People can surprise you. A devious mind is capable of more than we're comfortable admitting."

"You're right." Why did she feel so defeated as she said the words? What had she thought? That she'd prance into town and, when the time came, go back to

Seattle and seal the fate of the DH-7 members, only to live happily ever after when all was said and done?

She knew better than that.

Ty stood, wiped the sand from him, and offered his hand. "Let's go back inside. Austin should be here soon. I'll feel better when my truck is fixed, and we're not stranded here. Although being stranded with you has its appeal."

With ease that displayed his strength, Ty pulled Cassidy to her feet and practically into his arms. There were very few places she felt safe—but in Ty's embrace was one of those.

Lucy had been the only other person to accept Cassidy for who she was and not what she could give— and God had taken Lucy away.

Fear momentarily gripped Cassidy. What if God took away Ty as well?

She could hardly stomach the thought.

———

Just as they walked up to the lighthouse, Wes pulled up. Wes was another friend from Bible study, a part-time plumber and an anytime kayak guide. Summer was his busy season, which meant that Ty didn't see him as often.

Wes hopped out of his truck and walked toward them. His hair was cut short, matching the shadow of a beard across his jaw and upper lip. He was quiet, with a dry sense of humor and an adventurous spirit.

"Austin had something come up." Wes flipped his keys around his fingers. "So I came to give you a tow. The water is rough today, so I cancelled the kayak tour I had scheduled."

Ty extended his hand in brotherly comradery. "Good to see you, man. You've been a little too busy this summer."

Wes shrugged, that laidback island attitude ever present. "What can I say? Gotta make enough to pay my bills for the rest of the year. And I have to surf on occasion."

Surfers around here were known to set their own business hours, based solely on the forecast. Good surfing waves? Then work could wait until tomorrow. It was a different mind-set—one that made life more interesting.

"I hear you."

"Good to see you, Cassidy." Wes nodded her way. "So, what's going on?"

"Listen, while you two talk, I'm going inside for a minute and clear my head," Cassidy said.

"Do you want me to check it out first?" Ty asked, worry filling him.

"No, I'll be fine." Her gaze caught his and clearly communicated that she could check things out for herself.

He didn't argue. The woman was capable. No one could argue with that.

With one last glance back, Wes and Ty started walking toward his truck.

"So, what happened to the Big Kahuna?" Wes asked. He'd given Ty's truck her own name.

"I'm not sure," Ty said, remembering the earlier incident all too vividly. "One minute, everything was fine, and the next my brakes quit working."

"Did someone mess with them?" Wes narrowed his eyes.

"I don't think so, but I won't know for sure until I get it out of the sand and get a better look underneath."

"Let's get it done then."

It only took twenty minutes to tow the truck out from the deep, soft sand and to an old driveway outside the lighthouse. Once there, Ty scooted beneath the truck and used the flashlight Wes handed him to reexamine the brake line.

"So how does it look?" Wes asked, peering under the truck.

"Well, all the brake fluid is gone," he said. "There's a small cut in the line. Someone knew what they were doing."

"What do you mean?"

"They must have made an incision that was just small enough to get things rolling. As I was driving, the cut must have broken through and released the fluid."

"Makes sense. Otherwise, you would have seen a pool when you climbed in the truck."

"Exactly. The truck was going just fast enough it could have done some damage."

"These old beauties were built like tanks." Wes paused. "Why would someone tamper with your brakes? Does this have anything to do with Cassidy's ex-boyfriend?"

Ty pulled himself out from under the truck so he could see Wes's face. "You heard?"

"The gang told me. I ran into them when I stopped by the Chefette for a sandwich." He picked up a bag from his truck. "I brought you the supplies you asked for. I guess you anticipated this?"

"I suspected it." Ty took the bag. "And, yes, my first thought was that it could be this guy behind it. He's trouble."

"Sounds dangerous."

"He is." Ty frowned as he thought about it. He began pulling out the items he needed to fix his truck. "But we're trying not to jump to too many conclusions. She didn't get a good look at the man."

"I guess this explains why she seems so jumpy." Wes leaned against Big Kahuna.

Ty nodded. "Yeah, it answers a lot of questions."

They jacked the truck up and took the wheel off to begin repairs.

"I know we haven't caught up in a while, but the two of you seem like you've gotten close," Wes said.

Ty removed the old hose. "Yeah, we have."

"I'm happy for you, man. That's great. She seems like a really great gal."

She's going to leave you. Just like Renee. Just like your brother.

The voice had started whispering at the back of his mind earlier. He tried to silence it. But Ty would be a fool not to acknowledge the challenges he and Cassidy would face in the future. It wasn't just the distance either. It was career. Upbringing. Life goals.

Ty cleared his throat, pushing away those thoughts, and focused on repairing the truck. They worked for the next hour until the truck was as good as new. "Thanks for your help, man."

"It's no problem." Wes straightened and glanced at his watch. "Speaking of which, I should get back to work. Vacationers are very particular about their hot tubs not working."

"I can only imagine." If only that was Ty's biggest worry right now.

"If you need a hand with anything else, let me know."

"I'll do that. Thanks, Wes."

Ty waved goodbye to his friend and went to check on Cassidy, already uncomfortable with the amount of time he'd left her alone. She might be fully capable of taking care of herself, but that didn't mean he wanted her to do that. No, two people working together were always better than one person standing alone.

He'd push aside his apprehension about the future. He'd worry about that when the day came. For now, he'd stay focused on keeping the woman he loved safe.

CASSIDY STARED AT HER PHONE. She'd been trying to find any new information on Orion with no success. Nothing online indicated where he was or what he was doing now.

She'd figured that much, but it had been worth a try. And at least she'd been doing something, which beat sitting around wasting time. This day was almost over, the sun was beginning to set, and she was no closer to finding answers than she had been earlier.

No, she just had more questions.

She leaned back in the rickety kitchen chair and froze as a noise caught her ear.

What was that sound? A howl echoed in the background, the sound wispy and drawn out.

She reached for her gun, her heart pounding in her ears.

Another howl whispered throughout the building.

The wind, she realized. It was just the wind slicing

through the open window and circling up the lighthouse.

She scolded herself for being on edge. But who wouldn't be in this situation?

The sound was so eerie—almost otherworldly. Yet she didn't believe in ghosts.

Lantern Beach might start making her a believer.

For that matter, Elsa and this lighthouse should get along just fine.

Just as the thought hit her, something banged behind her.

Cassidy jumped, gripping her gun and ready to fight.

She twirled around and saw . . . Ty standing there.

Of course.

She bit back a laugh and lowered her gun. "Sorry."

"Didn't mean to scare you." Ty stepped closer and put his hands on his hips as he observed her. "The wind caught the door and slammed it shut."

Cassidy turned to face him and saw the sheen of sweat across his face. The smudge of grease on his hand. The heavy breathing of someone who'd been doing a laborious job.

He looked perfect. Just perfect.

She cleared her throat. "I don't usually say stuff like this, but this place is kind of freaking me out."

He chuckled and washed his hands in the kitchen sink. "What do you mean?"

"I mean, the wind keeps whipping through here

making this howling sound. I'm not superstitious. I'm really not. But this place feels a little eerie."

"Yeah, well there's a lot of history here. But this place has saved many lives."

"I know it has."

"My mom always says that God's Word is our lighthouse as we try to navigate the seas of life."

Cassidy smiled at the imagery. "I love your mom. She's very wise. And I agree with her assessment—more and more every day."

"That makes me happy." He hooked his arm around her neck and pulled her into a hug. "Listen, Mac said we could stay with him tonight. And since he has AC and a working bathroom, I figured that was a good idea."

"Sounds like a plan."

Twenty minutes later, they pulled up to Mac's house, a little bungalow located four houses from the ocean. They'd picked up Kujo on the way—the dog was always welcome at Mac's.

Cassidy had decided before she arrived to tell Mac the truth—all of it. If he was going to be involved, then he deserved to know the details of what he was getting into. More than that, she knew she could trust him.

Mac paused and stared at Cassidy when she stepped inside. The worry and concern in his expression made it clear he'd come to think of her like a daughter.

He stepped closer and squeezed her arm. "I'm glad you're here, Cassidy."

"Thanks for letting us come." Funny how these

people she'd only known for a couple months seemed to care about her more than people she'd known her entire life.

She glanced around his house, partially to discern if they'd interrupted anything. She nodded toward a row of small personal safes on his table. "You've been keeping yourself busy."

The man loved to polish up his police skills, sometimes going to the extreme. "What can I say? You never know when it might come in handy to crack a safe. Have a seat. Would you like a drink?"

"Some water would be great."

A few minutes later, they had their drinks and sat on the couch near each other. Cassidy told Mac everything she'd told Ty earlier, starting with her being a detective, moving to her undercover assignment, and concluding with how she'd ended up here.

Mac's eyes narrowed when she finished. "I knew there was more to your story and have been looking forward to the day you felt comfortable enough to share. God bless you, Cassidy, for everything you've done."

"Thank you." She nearly choked on her words. No, not her words. At Mac's words and the sincerity behind them. Her job had often been thankless. Her parents certainly hadn't admired her choices. She hadn't even realized how much she craved a pat on the back. But she had.

"So now we need to figure out a way to keep you

alive," he continued. "I can do that. First of all, are you sure this is the guy?"

Cassidy shook her head, replaying everything in her mind. "No, I'm not certain. I mean, he looked like Orion, but he wasn't dressed like him. Didn't walk like him. From what Lisa said, he didn't talk like Orion either."

"So that's the first thing we need to figure out," Mac said. "Is this really your guy?"

"I agree," Ty added. "If it's not Orion, then we resume life as normal. If it is Orion, then we need to keep in mind that he may not know for certain that you're here or where you live. He may have come here looking on a hunch."

"If it is him, then what?" Cassidy asked. "We ask him to leave?"

"We *make* him leave," Mac said. "I'm sure the police can find a reason to arrest him and put him away for a while."

"Can they find something provable?" Cassidy said, feeling like the solution was too simple. "That's the question. These guys are good at covering their tracks. As you both know, you can't be arrested for being in a gang. He's had his hand in drug deals, thefts, and even murder. But without evidence, it doesn't matter."

"Once a criminal, always a criminal," Mac said. "Not in every case, but it's true for someone like Orion. We'll keep our eyes on him. He'll mess up. Believe me."

Cassidy nodded. "I get that."

Mac looked around on his phone and then held it up. "This is what you really look like?"

Cassidy looked at the picture. She had dark hair. Straight. Pulled back in a bun. Pale skin and a professional-looking outfit.

It was quite the contrast to her current wavy blonde hair, sun-kissed complexion, and tank top.

"That's me," she said.

She almost didn't recognize whom she used to be. Even the look in her eyes in that photo . . . it was emptier somehow.

"You look different. That's good. I'd hardly recognize you."

"That's what I was aiming for."

"That should buy you some time," Mac said.

Ty's phone buzzed, and he glanced at the screen. "It's Wes. I sent him a picture of Orion a few minutes ago—he asked me to. He says he worked on a hot tub for a rental house. The guy staying there looked like Orion."

Cassidy's heart raced. "Where? Where is this house?"

Ty typed back and waited. A few seconds later, he had his answer.

"We need to go there." Cassidy rushed to her feet. "Now."

"WE CAN'T DO ANYTHING RASH," Ty said, standing and moving toward the door, almost like he was preparing to stop her from doing anything foolish.

"We won't—we'll observe," Cassidy said. "Watch. Verify."

Ty's phone buzzed again—this time over and over. Someone was calling.

He frowned when he saw the screen this time. "I forgot they were calling about the grant today."

Cassidy had forgotten too, but she knew how important this was. "You're going to have to hop online and do some paperwork during the call."

His jaw flexed. "I need to go with you."

"I'll go," Mac said. "I won't let her get in trouble. You can use my computer. I left it online."

Ty still hesitated. His phone continuing to ring. He was going to miss the call soon.

"You should answer," Cassidy told him. "This is important, Ty, and I promise I'll be careful."

Finally, he nodded. "Fine. But call me at the first sign of trouble."

Before he could change his mind and argue more, Cassidy started toward the door.

Maybe she'd figure out some answers. She could only hope.

She climbed in Mac's truck. Twilight had fallen, and the sky was the easy gray that came before the darkness of deep night surrounded them fully. Crickets chirped and frogs sang their strange songs from a pond not far away.

"Seattle detective, huh?" Mac said, stealing a glance at Cassidy from the corner of his eye as he headed down the road.

"I'm sorry I kept it from you."

"Oh, I get it. With investigation sometimes comes deceit. This couldn't have been easy on you."

She glanced at her hands, at the once pale skin now tinged an amazing shade of sun-kissed tan. She wished it was easier to put into words everything she was feeling. Her life had been turned upside down over these past few months, and she was only beginning to realize the emotional impact of that.

"It hasn't been," she said. "I don't like lying to the people I care about."

"Ty seems understanding."

"He's been amazing." She paused, her thoughts unsettled. "Were you ever married, Mac?"

He nodded. "Twelve years. Her name was Carol. Love of my life."

"Do you mind if I ask what happened?" The street blurred past around them, the darkness bringing a certain stillness with it.

His face tightened, and he frowned. "I lost her."

Cassidy instantly knew she'd crossed a line. "I'm sorry, Mac. I shouldn't have asked."

Instead of responding, he pointed to a house in the distance. "There it is."

He pulled to the side of the road. The cottage was located right off the highway. If they pulled in front of the house, they'd be too suspicious. But vacationers often parked on the side of the highway and walked to the beach.

Thankfully, the darkness concealed them.

Cassidy stared at the house. It was two stories. Probably twenty years old, if she had to guess, based on the style and upkeep. The outside appeared clean and neat.

A white, mid-sized SUV sat in the driveway. It looked classy and . . . normal.

Another moment of unease churned in her gut. The pieces just weren't fitting together. She was more desperate than ever to learn the truth.

"Now we just watch," Mac said. "If this is your guy, we don't want to show our hand."

"I agree." She crossed her arms. "Did you bring the coffee and donuts?"

Mac chuckled. "I like the way you think, Cassidy. But I didn't."

"Oh, man. Stakeouts are the worst." It felt good to say it, to speak truth and drop the pretenses.

"Aren't they, though? They always look so interesting on TV. In reality, it's hours and hours of doing almost nothing except attempting to stay awake."

"Amen."

"It is where I taught myself to recite the alphabet forward, backward, and skipping every other letter."

"I tried to memorize pi," she admitted.

"I think mine is better for entertaining folks."

"Good thing I never strove to be an entertainer." She smiled.

The lighthearted moment faded.

"Cassidy, it's good having someone like you around here," Mac said, sticking one of his signature toothpicks in his mouth. He kept extras in his shirt pocket, apparently. "Lantern Beach could use your expertise."

"They have you to guide them when Bozoman messes up." She glanced at him.

"Some new blood would be nice, though." There wasn't even a hint of teasing in his voice.

"I don't know, Mac. I always assumed I'd resume life in Seattle."

"It's never too late for your life to take a different direction. In fact, that's exactly what we need sometimes. We need to recalculate and reevaluate. We've only got one chance to make this right."

"You're right." What did that look like for Cassidy? She wasn't sure any more.

"Besides, I don't think Ty is prepared for you to leave. You've been good for him."

"I have a lot to think about, that's for sure." She leaned back and stared at the house. "I need to figure the Orion situation out before I worry about that."

"He's a pretty bad guy, huh?"

"Mac, I'd never seen such evil until I went undercover with DH-7. They have no regard for human life. Just thinking about them, about my time undercover . . . it chills me to the bone. And that means a lot coming from an urban detective."

"Here's a little known fact. I worked for eight years as a cop in Atlanta."

"Did you? I had no clue." Mac didn't talk about his past much—mostly in jest. But she'd been curious about his history.

"I did. I thought I would get bored around here in such a small town. But it helped restore my faith in humanity. There are good people. And troublemakers. Of course. But I don't need excitement surrounding me to make life interesting. We're in charge of choosing what's interesting. Boring people think it's an external thing, and they try to hide just how boring they are by doing interesting things."

She smiled at his apt description. "I like the way you think."

Silence ticked between them a minute.

"I met my Carol in Atlanta."

Cassidy sucked in a quick breath, grateful that Mac trusted her enough to share. "Did you?"

"She was the most beautiful woman I'd ever laid eyes on." His gaze took on a glow Cassidy hadn't seen before.

"I bet she was special if she fell in love with you and vice versa."

"Hey—what's that mean?"

"It was a compliment. No offense."

"No offense taken. Just giving you a hard time." He chuckled again but the sound faded, and he drew in a deep breath. "Marrying her was one of the happiest days of my life."

Cassidy's heart warmed. She hoped that whomever she married some day would say the same about her. And she was increasingly thankful she hadn't married Ryan and perpetuated a cycle of workaholism combined with lackluster passion in her life.

Ty's image came to mind instead. Could he be the one? She supposed it was too early to tell.

"I wish I could have met Carol," Cassidy said finally.

"It was actually her idea to come here, you know," Mac said. "I was involved in a case. The bad guy grabbed me, put the gun to my head, and I wasn't sure I was going to make it out of the situation alive."

"Sounds scary."

"It was. Carol didn't like the thought of losing me and becoming a widow. So we came here when I was thirty. We were still newlyweds. Wanted to start a family, but we didn't think it was going to happen. She finally got pregnant. We were over-the-moon happy."

Cassidy braced herself for the outcome of this story. Based on the wistfulness in his voice, it wasn't a happy one. "I bet."

"She died in childbirth." His voice went placid with grief. "They tried to save the baby. Baby Grace. She survived for forty-nine whole minutes. That girl was a fighter."

"Just like her dad." Cassidy's voice broke as she said the words.

"Yeah, just like her dad." His voice trailed with emotion, as the past surfaced and his words swept him back in time.

"I'm sorry, Mac."

He seemed to snap from his grief and pull himself together. "That was a long time ago. Life goes on. As hard as it was, I was blessed with the years I had with Carol. I was blessed by the forty-nine minutes Grace lived, and the nine months her mother carried her in the womb. Life is full of different chapters, and the sooner we learn to accept that, the better."

"I can't deny that," Cassidy said. "Sometimes you have to read through to the end, even the chapters you don't like."

Del's voice sounded in Cassidy's head. *As believers, we know the ending, though. Don't we?*

Cassidy was so glad she'd met people who weren't afraid to let her explore the idea of faith in her own life. She'd always been curious about it, but her family had marked off religion as nonsense. The more Cassidy prayed and read her Bible, the more she realized it was far from nonsense. She also realized that church was more than a gang of Bible-believing folks who came together every week for a social club. Faith and the actions that followed were things that sustained you through your darkest days.

Mac straightened and nodded across the street. "There's our guy, Cassidy."

Her eyes zeroed in on the man leaving his house and climbing into the SUV. "We've got to follow him."

THEY PULLED to a stop at the General Store, parking several spaces over from Orion's white SUV. Cassidy sat back, hating the uncertainty of who this man really was and what he was doing here.

"You should go in," Cassidy said.

"I can't leave you." Mac's eyes never left Orion.

"I'm watching the man from here. I'll lock the doors. Everything will be fine. Grab some donuts and coffee while you're in there."

He chuckled. "There's that humor again. You want me to talk to him?"

"I want you to follow your instincts—whatever that leads you to do."

He sat silently a minute before grabbing the silver handle beside him. "Okay. Let me see what I can find out. Lock the doors."

As soon as Mac was out, Cassidy did as he'd asked.

And then she sat back and waited, watching everything through the big glass windows at the front of the store.

Orion paced the aisle, as if on a mission. He stopped by the medication section.

Cassidy studied him from afar, her gut twisting. He looked so much like Orion—except for the way he dressed and carried himself. It just didn't make any sense.

And she hated it when things didn't make sense.

Mac walked into the store and headed to the same aisle. He grabbed something from the shelf and turned to mutter something to Orion.

Orion smiled in response and said something that appeared lighthearted.

The two men walked toward the register together, still chatting.

What Cassidy wouldn't give to hear what they were saying.

Instead, she had to watch and wait.

Finally, Orion stepped outside, waved goodbye to Mac, and went to his SUV. He didn't even glance over at Cassidy as he climbed into his vehicle and took off down the road.

Five minutes later, Mac climbed back inside with two cups of coffee, two donuts and . . . a bottle of TUMS?

"Digestive system isn't what it used to be," he muttered, locking his door.

Cassidy waited for him to continue. Any other time,

she'd add something witty. She wasn't in the mood now.

"I don't know, Cassidy." He narrowed his eyes until a fan of wrinkles appeared at their edges. "He didn't do anything that raised any flags in my mind. He gave me the same story he gave Lisa. He and his wife were married here. She died. He's here on their anniversary, just spending some time in reflection."

Cassidy's stomach clenched. She'd expected that, yet she'd hoped for more. "What was he buying?"

"Some aloe. Said he got some sunburn today and that it was bothering him."

She let her head fall back into the seat. None of that was what she wanted to hear. She needed something definitive. She needed *answers*.

"What are you thinking, Mac?" she finally said, desperate for another opinion. A professional one she could trust.

He let out a sigh and stared out the window. "Several years ago, I went to the Florida Keys on vacation. While I was there, I saw my brother."

"Okay . . ." She had no idea where he was going with this.

"Well, it wasn't actually my brother. But the man was his doppelganger. It was insane how much they looked alike."

And suddenly Cassidy knew exactly what he was saying. "So you think everyone in the world has a twin?"

Mac shrugged. "Maybe."

"And you think this guy isn't actually Orion?"

"I'm not ruling anything out. I'm just trying to keep an open mind. Isn't that one of the first things we're taught as detectives? That we have to take our blinders off?"

She nodded, unable to argue. "It is. And, honestly, I'm confused about this whole situation."

"We'll find some answers, Cassidy. Just be patient. In the meantime, I'll call a realtor friend of mine. See if I can find out who's renting that house. Maybe it will give us some kind of clue."

"How did the call go?" Cassidy asked Ty as soon as they got back to Mac's place. She'd texted him to let him know they were on the way. There was no need to stay longer—Orion, or whoever he was—was probably in for the night.

"It went fine." Ty studied her—something he did a lot. The ever-perceptive veteran had an affinity for trying to figure her out. "Great, actually. But I don't want to talk about that now. How did your stakeout go?"

Cassidy and Mac updated him on what had happened—over donuts and coffee, of course.

"So we still don't know anything more?" Ty said, a touch of exhaustion in his voice.

"Pretty much," Mac said. "But Cassidy and I got to talk. That was something."

"It was," Cassidy agreed.

"But we still need a plan," Ty said.

"Can we look into marriage records here on the island?" Cassidy said. "See if this guy really did get married three years ago? That would answer some questions."

"Any marriage licenses should be on record, but it's going to take some time," Mac said. "I can look into it tomorrow, if you'd like."

"If you wouldn't mind . . ."

"Darling, you know I live for stuff like this. Of course, I don't mind." Mac shifted. "Ty, why don't you and I take shifts tonight keeping a lookout?"

"Oh, no," Cassidy said. "You're not leaving me out of this. No way will I sit back like a damsel in distress."

"Somehow I had a feeling you'd say that." Mac grinned. "How about if I take the first shift? I have a few more combinations to crack. I bought those all at the thrift store. I put my favorite guns inside, and unless I crack the combo, I won't get them back."

Mac's antics never failed to entertain Cassidy, even in the most dire situations.

"It's a plan," Cassidy said. "Thanks for letting us stay here."

"Any time, Cassidy. You can take the bedroom on the left. Ty, you've got the couch."

"Sounds good," Ty said. "I'll take second shift."

"I think I'm going to turn in for the night," Cassidy said. "It's been a long day."

"You can say that again," Mac said. "Goodnight."

"I'll walk you to your room," Ty said.

He placed a hand on her back as they went down the hallway and paused outside her door. Ty stepped closer and tenderly kissed her forehead before wrapping her in his arms.

"Goodnight, Cassidy." His voice sounded tender and full of deep emotion.

Cassidy held on to Ty, halfway not wanting to let go. Their month of blissful dating was disappearing, replaced with stress and urgency. "Goodnight. Thank you for everything."

Ty's gaze locked with Cassidy's, a husky look lingering in the depths of his eyes. He reached for her, his hands cradling her face and something unsaid in his eyes. Before she could ask him about it, his lips met hers. Claimed her. Swept her away from her problems and into another world. A welcome escape.

But there was something more to the lip lock—something deeper.

When Ty stepped back, Cassidy could hardly breathe and her heart raced with adrenaline. She touched her lips, still trying to find her balance.

"Why did that feel like a goodbye kiss?" Cassidy whispered.

"What do you mean?" Ty's voice sounded as raspy as his gaze was smoky.

"You accused me of giving you a goodbye kiss earlier. Now I understand it. Something about that kiss felt final, for some reason." Cassidy's heart lurched into her throat at the thought.

Had Ty come to his senses? Realized how difficult dating her was? Figured all this trouble wasn't worth it?

"You're reading too much into it," he murmured.

But was she? Because she had a feeling something was going on in Ty's mind, something he wasn't talking about.

She'd give him time. But she didn't like where her thoughts were headed.

"SO, how are we going to handle this?" Cady asked Orion.

He'd insisted on driving his flashy black BMW, a vehicle that he had blinged-out to the max. Leather seats. Fancy rims. A sound system that exceeded what seemed necessary for a mere car and more appropriate for a concert.

"We're going to find Reginald, tell him what's up, and then finish him," Orion said, speaking as casually as a person talking about a to-do list around the house. "It's that easy."

"Finish him how?" Cady's voice cracked, a telltale sign of her nerves.

She had to get them under control. But they were talking about ending someone's life here. And she didn't have a backup plan.

She still had no idea how she was going to get out of this—and Cady always had a plan. Her dad used to say she was born with both a plan and a good dose of stubbornness. She couldn't argue.

"We'll finish him however seems like the most fun at the moment." A touch of amusement lilted Orion's voice. "I've got my gun—that's not usually fun. I also brought a knife, a lighter, and some Clorox. Now those things could make this more interesting."

Cady's stomach squeezed with nausea.

No, no, no . . .

She had to figure this out somehow.

Orion pressed harder on the accelerator. He had to be going twenty miles over the speed limit. That was Orion. He lived fast and hard, almost as if he was invincible.

"Why are you so nervous?" Orion glanced over at her. "You've killed before."

No, Cady hadn't killed before, even though everyone within DH-7 believed she had. It had all been a setup, an illusion, an elaborate ploy.

"You don't get nervous?" she asked, deflecting the question.

"Nah. What's there to be nervous about? Reginald knew the consequences he'd face when he left us. He's getting what he has coming to him. You can't be hardcore and scared."

There was a challenge in the statement, and Cady knew he was waiting for her to explain herself.

"I'm prepared to do whatever necessary to ensure my place in DH-7. I don't know what else you want me to say." She hardened her voice just enough to sound convincing.

He glanced at her too long, considering their speed. "Raul likes you."

"That's good."

"I don't get it."

"I'm sorry to hear that." She could hear the suspicion in his voice, and it put her on edge.

"Where did you come from?"

Anxiety clogged her throat. If Orion had the whim, he'd kill Cady too. But he'd torture her for answers first.

"I've been over this before," she finally said. "It's not important."

"It is to me. If we're going to do this together, I need to know I can trust you."

Cady raised her chin, not giving into the argument Orion was so desperately trying to start. "I haven't let Raul down yet."

"And that's a good thing. I'd give my life for him."

"Loyalty like yours doesn't come around often."

"Yeah, well, he gave my life purpose."

Was that what all of this boiled down to? Purpose?

Gang members were people who were often lost and neglected, trying to find their place in the world. Acceptance from these groups—however evil they were—gave them a sense of fulfillment. Cady had taken classes on it. But seeing this study in real life chilled her blood.

They were like a cult—a young, urban cult with individuals willing to drink the Kool-Aid or to die so Haley's

Comet could sweep them into space. The desperation existed in every walk of life—rich or poor, young or old. It existed across races and paychecks and belief systems.

Purpose and belonging carried a huge weight in people's lives.

There had to be a better way.

"I killed Alisha," he muttered.

Cady drew in a deep breath, certain she hadn't heard him correctly. "What?"

"Alisha," he said. "You know who she is."

"Your girlfriend?" Cady had seen her just a few days ago.

"Raul decided he didn't like her."

Her heart pounded in her ears. "So you killed her?"

Cassidy tried to hide her disgust, but it was difficult.

"She may have tipped off members of the Blood Brotherhood. We couldn't risk it. We don't show mercy to traitors."

Orion's words served as a stark, cold reminder of what could be Cady's future if she wasn't careful.

She felt the need to say something to prove her own loyalty, but her thoughts felt scrambled. Finally, she cleared her throat, trying to erase the chilling images that filled her mind.

"I've been on the streets—on my own—since I was twelve," she said, recalling her cover story. "So for a lot of years. I almost took my own life because I had nothing to live for. No way to get ahead. The rest of my life stretched out like one long, bleak road before me, and I had no hope."

"Is that right?"

"Then I met Raul a couple months ago. He took me in. He not only gave me food and shelter, but he gave me a sense of purpose. Now I'm just trying to repay him."

Orion grunted, as if unsure he believed her story. Before he could ask any more questions, he pulled to a stop in front of a dumpy looking house in a drab neighborhood known for crime, drugs, and prostitution. The police debriefed on this area daily, and it was often mentioned in the news since a new crime was committed here every night.

"We're here," he announced.

Another swell of anxiety swirled in Cady.

She was going to have to rely on that instinct now and play this by ear. Not her first choice—or the best one. It was her only choice.

"Come on," Orion said.

Before she could feign an excuse, he was out of the car and skulking toward a house across the street. A single light lit the window.

Someone appeared to be home.

And now Cady was going to have to improvise before she did something reprehensible.

CHAPTER
FOURTEEN

TODAY'S GOALS: USE WISDOM.
STAY ALIVE. WIN.

CASSIDY TOOK the last shift of the evening and spent her time not only on guard duty, but also poring over online news articles on DH-7 and all their recent mayhem. There were car thefts. Drug deals. Drive-by shootings. Nothing surprising.

Again.

She wasn't sure what she hoped to find, but her brain wouldn't stop working until she had some answers. Not knowing if it was really Orion in town was driving her crazy.

She leaned back in the kitchen chair where she'd settled and glanced back into the living room. Ty snoozed on the couch. Cassidy smiled as she watched him. One arm was thrown over his head. His face looked relaxed and unaware. His breathing was even and deep.

She could imagine spending the rest of her life seeing him in the morning—bedhead, sleepy eyes, and all. She liked the idea a little too much, especially considering the fact that she was in no position to plan the rest of her life. All she needed to concentrate on right now was surviving.

Their kiss last night slammed into her mind again. What had been the emotion behind it? Cassidy still wasn't sure, but she'd mulled it over all evening. Yesterday must have been a wake-up call for Ty. She just wasn't sure what the new reality he was facing looked like.

A sound at the end of the hallway drew her attention. Mac appeared from his bedroom, dressed and looking as perky as ever as he ambled toward her. "Morning. No trouble?"

"No trouble. I did brew some fresh coffee."

"Perfect. You two can hide out here anytime." He glanced down. "You too, Kujo."

She smiled and patted the dog's head. "Anything new?"

"My realtor friend called me back. Turns out the person renting that house is named Rich and he's from Missouri. It's a last-minute reservation—he called three days ago and asked what was available. Said he'd take whatever they had."

"That fits our theory. It would be different if it was someone who'd booked months in advance."

"Exactly."

"Since you're up, do you mind if I have a minute? I desperately need a shower." Thankfully, she'd brought her bags with her.

"Well . . . I wasn't going to say anything." He cackled at his own joke. "Just kidding, of course. Go right ahead."

By the time Cassidy finished getting ready, Ty was up and drinking coffee with Mac. After a few pleasantries, she glanced at her watch. "We have forty minutes until church starts."

Ty lowered his cup. "You're right. Let me get ready."

Mac stood. "Speaking of which, I'm late for my service. You two gonna be okay?"

"Of course," Ty said. "We'll check in later."

Cassidy grabbed an apple to eat as she waited. Ty appeared a few minutes later, looking clean and smelling like a rain shower. He must have borrowed Mac's shampoo.

She'd been going with Ty to a small church on the edge of the town. The building itself was picturesque, with its white shingles, tall steeple, and stained-glass windows. Its history went back more than two hundred years, and Cassidy could just imagine people from decades ago sitting on these wooden pews and singing hymns as they braved the elements out here, minus the conveniences of modern life.

Today, the church had two services. The first was traditional and strictly hymns. The second utilized a praise band and more casual atmosphere.

Either way, the gathering was small. In the summertime, half the congregants were visitors. Cassidy hadn't been here during the winter, but Ty had told her that it usually ran about thirty people on an average Sunday.

This was where he and the rest of the gang had first met. They'd started a Bible study together, but it was currently on hiatus for the summer because of the crazy schedules in this area and their respective businesses.

Cassidy had been attending the past month, and she'd surprised herself by liking it.

She hadn't thought a lot of church or religion while growing up. Partly because of her wealthy upbringing —she'd wanted for nothing and had no need for reliance on God. Then when Lucy was murdered, she figured if there was a God out there, He wasn't loving.

But, after infiltrating DH-7, she'd seen the need for people to find purpose and belonging in their lives. This church offered both of those things—yet it offered so much more. It offered answers, answers that fascinated her, and answers that had turned her life around in more than one way.

They took a seat beside Austin and Skye at the back of the sanctuary and made small talk.

As a shadow fell over them, Cassidy looked up. Jimmy James stood there wearing his best torn jeans and stained white T-shirt. The service was come as you are, so no one here would complain.

"Hey," he grunted. "I just got called into work, so I can't stay. But I wanted to let you know I saw that guy again last night."

Jimmy James suddenly had her full attention. "Is that right?"

As he nodded, the skin of his thick neck folded into

rolls. "I didn't have a chance to talk to him, but I'm pretty sure it was the same man."

"What time was it?" Cassidy and Mac had staked out his place from eight until around ten.

"I don't know. Probably eleven? I was working late." He shrugged and lifted his eyebrows. "On my business."

On the knockoff purses, he meant.

Eleven o'clock? It could have been Orion.

"Did anything unusual happen?" Ty asked.

Jimmy James shrugged again. "Unusual? Not really. But there was a woman with him this time."

A woman? What sense did that make? "What did she look like?"

"Hard to say. Long hair. Dark. She seemed to be there willingly." He paused. "I know that doesn't help a lot, but I figured you'd want to know."

"Thanks, Jimmy James," Cassidy said. "I appreciate it. And it does help."

As the band started—Wes on drums and Lisa playing keyboard—Cassidy reflected on what Jimmy James had said. Who could the woman be? Cassidy certainly hadn't seen a woman with Orion, nor had anyone else mentioned one.

She'd have to ask Wes if there was another woman at the man's house when he'd gone to work on the hot tub. It seemed as if he would have mentioned that.

In the middle of the first song, "This Is Amazing Grace," someone walked into the service late and took a seat across the aisle.

Cassidy peeked over, and her mouth gaped.

It was Orion.

He'd come to church.

———

Ty's muscles bristled, and he slipped an arm around Cassidy's shoulders as his instincts flared to life.

Had Orion come here to mock Cassidy? To tease her? Intimidate her?

It didn't matter the reason. Ty didn't like it. He'd make sure to remain between Cassidy and the island's most intriguing visitor.

Cassidy might be capable, but that didn't tamp down his urge to protect her.

"Do you want to leave?" Ty whispered, leaning close enough that her hair tickled his face.

Cassidy shook her head, but her stiff jaw clearly said it all. She was on edge. "No. If Orion already knows I'm here on Lantern Beach, there's no need to run away."

He had to admire her bravery. But it was a fine line between bravery and stupidity. They had to err on the side of caution. If he pushed too hard, Cassidy would only resent him.

Ty glanced back over. The man did appear normal, dressed in casual attire. He didn't see any tattoos or piercings or anything else that would signal a dangerous history.

Ty didn't like this, and he fought the urge to confront the man and demand answers.

Not here. Not now. And not if it meant putting Cassidy in a precarious position.

Ty couldn't concentrate for the entire service. No, he kept examining the man.

What kind of gang leader came to church? Dressed in a light-blue shirt with a pastel tie? Sang like he was familiar with the songs?

Ty knew Cassidy was conflicted about what was going on, and he couldn't blame her. He was conflicted as well.

Either this guy was a great actor or he wasn't Orion. But what were the chances that someone who looked just like the man would show up here?

"So we've got to learn to let go of things here on this earth, to not hold too tightly to what we think we love," Pastor Caleb said.

Not to hold too tightly . . . the reminder brought him back to his future with Cassidy. She'd warned him when they started dating that she couldn't make any promises about the future. He'd told himself he was okay with that.

But now it didn't feel okay. The only thing that felt okay was a future where the two of them ended up together.

Orion threatened that.

As the invitation song drew near, Wes and Lisa went back onstage to play. Ty whispered to Austin what was going on. Austin glanced back, and his eyes widened.

"That takes a lot of nerve," Austin said. "You want me to step in?"

Ty shook his head. "We're in church—this isn't the place for a scene."

The man had probably known that. This was the perfect place to show up, get close to Cassidy, and send a clear message without the threat of anyone calling him out.

"I could sic Mabel on him," Austin whispered. "She'll keep him talking for hours and have him plugged in as an usher within ten minutes of the end of the service. That could buy you some time."

"Let's keep her out of it." Although, Ty liked the way his friend thought. Ms. Mabel was a talker, for sure, and a fixture here at the church.

Before the last song ended, Ty stood. He wanted to get Cassidy out of here. Now.

He guided her from the pew to the exit and all the way to his truck. Distance from the man was the wisest decision right now.

Before they could climb inside, someone behind them said, "Excuse me."

Ty looked back. Just as he suspected.

It was Orion.

"What do you want me to do?" Ty whispered.

"Talk to him," Cassidy said, her expression pensive. "Don't hint at anything. I want to see how he plays this."

Ty wasn't sure about this. He preferred the direct route himself. But he admired the fact Cassidy wanted to confront her problems head on.

"Good morning." Ty turned to talk face-to-face, trying to keep the simmering anger from his voice.

Cassidy slipped behind him, partially concealing her face, and slid on her sunglasses.

"You dropped this." Orion held out a bulletin. "It has sermon notes, so I thought it could be important."

Ty reached for it, the unease in his gut growing by the moment. "Thank you. You must be from out of town."

Orion nodded. "I am. Missouri. I've really enjoyed being here. Lantern Beach is a great place."

Ty fought to keep his voice even. "Enjoy your stay."

"Oh, I will. I'm finally going to get some closure."

Fire lit in Ty, but before he could say anything, Orion continued.

"My wife died, so I came to celebrate the brief years we had together," he said.

Ty tamped down his reply and instead said, "I'm sorry to hear that."

Orion nodded at them before walking away.

Ty's shoulders relaxed. He'd watched the man's face and hadn't seen a hint of recognition.

Something strange was going on here, and he didn't like it. And, just like Cassidy, he wasn't sure of the best way to get to the bottom of it.

CASSIDY'S HEART raced as she climbed into Ty's truck. She waited until the doors were shut before daring to speak. She could feel her breaths coming too rapidly, the sweat spreading across her forehead, the frantic pace of her thoughts.

"Ty, he looks just like him." She watched Orion's white SUV pull away.

She was tempted to urge Ty to follow, but it would do no good. Orion was too smart for that.

If it was Orion.

If it wasn't him, then they'd just be stalking an innocent man. The sad fact remained that Cassidy was conflicted. Being conflicted went against everything she was trained to be—by both her father and by the police department.

"Is there anything distinguishing about Orion that will help us determine without a doubt it's him?"

"Orion had a lightning tattoo behind his ear." She

touched her own tattoo, her stomach roiling. She hadn't intended on getting it, but Raul had drugged her, and she'd woken up with the design permanently inked on her skin.

"I looked for a tattoo, but I didn't see one," Ty said.

"He could have put makeup over it," she muttered. Maybe she was grasping at straws here. Maybe she was losing it, and the stress of everything that had happened over the past few months was finally catching up to her. It was hard to tell which end was up at the moment.

"It's a possibility that Orion used some cover-up to conceal it," Ty said. "But we also need to remember that the man didn't act like he recognized you."

"I know." A sense of melancholy settled over Cassidy. "What does all of this even mean?"

"I have no idea. I hate to say it, but I feel a little lost right now too. Part of me wants to call him out on all this."

"We can't. If it is him, he'll just play dumb. If that's truly Orion, this is all some kind of elaborate mental game to him—including him showing up at church." She sighed. "I keep hoping things will come into focus, but they haven't."

"You know what they say?"

"Actually, I don't."

"If things don't come into focus, change your perspective."

"How do you suggest we do that? How can I look at this from a different angle? Ty, Orion killed his girlfriend because he thought she was sharing secrets with an opposing gang. He's one of the most dangerous men I've ever met. I can't stick my head in the sand."

"I'm not suggesting that. I'm only suggesting that we continue with what we're doing—keeping our eyes open, researching, talking to people. We'll find some answers eventually."

Cassidy released the pent-up air from her lungs. "You're right. I'm sorry. Everything is getting to me."

Ty squeezed her hand. "It's okay. I think you're doing remarkably well."

His tender voice made Cassidy want to curl up into a ball and bury herself in his embrace. She couldn't do that. She didn't have that luxury right now.

"Thank you, Ty. I don't know how I would have gotten through all this so far without you."

He kissed her hand softly. "You're worth fighting for, Cassidy."

Her cheeks heated at the sincerity of his words. She cleared her throat, ignoring the impulse she had to kiss him and forget all her problems. That wouldn't do anyone any good.

"Look, could we swing past my place?" she asked instead. "I need to grab some more clothes."

"Of course."

When they pulled up, Cassidy immediately noticed that Elsa was missing, and Serena's car was here instead.

Cassidy glanced at her phone and saw she'd gotten a text message from Serena during church.

> I know you're busy. Decided to help sell ice cream. Hope that's okay. Need the cash. SLAP? TIA

"Slap?" she asked.

"Sound like a plan?" Ty suggested.

"TIA?"

"Thanks in advance?"

"You're better at this than I realized."

"I had some time to read last night while I took my shift. I found a great article on texting 101."

Cassidy nodded then sighed and looked back at her phone. She knew she shouldn't have given Serena her own key to the ice cream truck. "Let me call her. This isn't the best time for her to take initiative. Not with everything going on."

Serena answered on the second ring. "Turkey in the Straw" played in the background and a laugh faded, along with the end of another conversation. "Enjoy that popsicle. It's the bomb. And if you hear 'Who Let the Dogs Out?,' free ice cream sandwiches on me."

As far as Cassidy knew, "Who Let the Dogs Out?" wasn't one of Elsa's songs.

"I was wondering when you'd call," Serena said.

Cassidy got right to the point. "You shouldn't have taken Elsa out, Serena. There's a lot happening right now."

"We're missing some great sales. I figured I'd help us both out by earning some cash. I *have* to work three jobs to make ends meet. Did I mention that?"

Cassidy felt for the girl. She really did. And she could understand the struggle to make ends meet. But . . . "Serena, there's a man who—"

"I know. Skye told me. I'll keep my eyes open for trouble."

Cassidy's gut twisted. It wasn't exactly that easy. "When you see trouble, it will be too late."

"Cassidy, I've got this. Anyone with two eyes can see we look nothing alike. No one will mistake me for you."

"That's beside the point. I need you to come back. Please." She added the *please* to be polite. Her next step would be to use her bossy cop voice.

Serena sighed. "Okay. Fine. I was just trying to help. I'll bring Elsa back and see if I can get more hours in with my aunt at the produce stand instead."

"Thank you. Come back. Now."

Serena sighed again. "Fine. Now."

"Thanks, Serena." Cassidy hit End and turned toward Ty. "She has good intentions but . . ."

"It's a good thing you told her to come back. Better safe than sorry."

————

Ty and Cassidy attempted to grab lunch at the Crazy Chefette, but there was an hour wait. Apparently, people were going crazy over today's special—lemon drop buffalo wings.

Instead, Ty and Cassidy ate at their second favorite

restaurant, a place called The Docks. It was located on the boardwalk and had great views of the ocean as well as a cozy coastal ambiance. The hustling crowds within view on the boardwalk made for good people watching. In the evening, string lights sparkled overhead.

The local town singer/songwriter, Carter Denver, was there offering entertainment. At the moment, he sang "Stand by Me." The song seemed appropriate.

Then again, the man seemed to have some kind of intuitive insight into Cassidy's life and always played songs that matched her current situation. She ordered a salad with shrimp, and Ty got crab cakes, his favorite.

Her thoughts were heavy. She was on the verge of quitting—not her relationship with Ty. No, her suspicions about Orion. What if she had this all wrong?

That's what it was all looking like.

Use obstacles as motivation to push harder.

The Day-at-a-Glance advice slammed into her mind. She wished she had more clarity now. She had plenty of obstacles and plenty of motivation. What she didn't have was answers.

"Okay, I've been thinking this through," Ty said, after taking a sip of his water.

"Please share." Maybe he had some insight to help.

"Let's talk this through from the beginning. First, you thought you saw Orion. That's what set all this off."

Memories of that first sighting filled Cassidy's thoughts, making her feel a little lightheaded. "That's correct."

"Then we learn some guy down at the docks was asking about you. This same guy was spotted again with a woman. That may or may not have anything to do with this."

"Also correct."

"Then my brake line is mysteriously cut. Your house is mysteriously broken into. And this guy mysteriously shows up at the very same church service that you attend."

"That's a lot of mysteriously-s."

Ty frowned. "Yes, it is. Too many."

Cassidy shifted, angling away from the overhead sun, which felt like a heat lamp this afternoon. "It does seem like a lot of coincidences."

He locked gazes with her, his eyes dead serious and no-nonsense. "He's got to be our guy, Cassidy."

Her heart spiked. Maybe Ty didn't think she was crazy after all. But that still didn't answer any of her questions. "What if he is? Then what do we do? Confront him?"

"We could slip a hint to the police chief."

"What do you mean?"

"We can have Bozeman be on the lookout for anything illegal. The first time Orion has a parking violation or speeds or does anything remotely illegal, the chief or one of his guys can arrest him. Search his things and maybe find evidence of his true motive for being in town. Gangbangers aren't known for registering their weapons. If he has an illegal gun, that's a great reason to lock him up. I'm sure the chief could find something."

"You may be right." It wasn't a bad idea, and it could work. Her first instinct was to have a more assertive plan, though.

Ty crossed his arms and gazed across the tables toward the boardwalk. "We can keep your name out of this. I can tell the chief that I heard a rumor."

She twirled her straw in the glass. "You really think that will work?"

"I think that's our best option right now, Cassidy. We've identified him. We've heard his cover story. We know he's fearless. Why else would he stop us in the church parking lot?"

She shivered. She'd thought the exact same thing. "You're right. He is."

"When we finish here, I'll go to the police station."

She thought about it a moment before nodding. When she set her emotions aside, she realized a subtle plan was better than the aggressive one she desired. "You're right. I think that is our best option. It sure beats confronting Orion. That wouldn't end well—for any of us."

"I agree. We've got to use our heads here. We've got to keep cool heads, for that matter."

With that settled, their food came, and they ate. But the air between them still felt heavy, despite their attempts at casual conversation.

Before they finished eating, a song floated toward them.

Cassidy paused, her senses going on alert.

Was that . . . "Who Let the Dogs Out?"

She and Ty exchanged a look.

It *was* that song. And it was coming from something that sounded strangely like Elsa.

———

Ty dropped some cash on the table before they hurried through the crowds. They scrambled down the boardwalk, trying to find the source of the music.

They were headed in the right direction because the song was getting louder. And they were walking past people eating frozen treats—the ones Cassidy stocked in her ice cream truck.

It didn't look like Serena had gone back to the house after all.

Irritation rushed up Cassidy's spine as she dodged more people.

She'd known the girl was stubborn, but Cassidy didn't think she would take it this far. Had Serena programmed this song into the ice cream truck? Because Cassidy was certain it wasn't a part of the musical lineup pre-programmed into Elsa.

"Where is the truck?" Ty muttered. "I hear it, but I don't see it anywhere."

"Good question." She glanced around. Ty was right. It sounded like they were close enough to touch it, yet neither saw it.

They cut through an alley toward the main highway.

As soon as they emerged on the other side, Elsa came into view. The pink truck was in a parking lot, music cheerily blaring.

But the crowds had thinned.

And Serena was nowhere in sight.

Cassidy stormed toward the vehicle, ready to give Serena a piece of her mind.

But when she peered inside, the truck was empty.

"Where is she?" Cassidy muttered.

Ty glanced around. "Did she just leave the ice cream truck with the music playing?"

"I knew she could be irresponsible, but I never thought it would go this far." This was totally coming out of Serena's paycheck. Cassidy had never agreed to give away free ice cream like this.

She reached inside and turned the music off before looking around again. Seriously—how far could the girl have gone since this song started playing?

Before she could search the parking lot, screams sounded in the distance. Ty and Cassidy glanced at each other before they hurried back toward the boardwalk, trying to see what was wrong.

When they reached the escalating crowds, Cassidy squinted, unsure if her eyes were deceiving her.

Three men were coming down the boardwalk. They were foaming at the mouth, flailing wildly, and looking all-together rabid.

In fact, some people might say they looked like . . . zombies.

CHAPTER
SIXTEEN

"CASSIDY?" Ty asked, looking as shocked as she felt.

She shook her head, unable to believe what she was seeing. "It's flakka, Ty. It's gotta be."

Flakka was the newest designer drug—and DH-7 had their hand in it. It was just recently beginning to reach the East Coast. But the psychedelic drug made most users lose their minds—and any good sense they had.

Some people gnawed their own flesh off. They hissed. They were a danger not only to themselves, but to others as well.

"Those guys are weirding me out," Ty said. "And I've seen some scary guys."

Cassidy watched as one of the "zombies" got on all fours, acting almost like a lion, and went after a teenage girl. She screamed and tried to run away.

But he caught her leg.

Ty darted toward them. He was faster than Cassidy —and stronger.

He reached the girl, but the man held onto her leg. Ty punched him in the face until the blond guy let go and staggered backward.

The girl crawled away. Cassidy grabbed her, pulling her into a nearby T-shirt store, where she'd be safe.

"Everyone, clear the area," Cassidy yelled, wondering why people were sticking around, waiting to become victims themselves.

Tourists scrambled to get away. A few remained with their cell phones raised. A couple remained frozen in shock where they stood.

The blond guy looked dazed as he crouched in front of Ty. Ty stood on guard, his body poised to fight back, if necessary.

With a quick shake, the blond sprang back to life and squatted in front of Ty. He hissed again, the sound sending a shiver up Cassidy's spine.

Cassidy held her breath, watching for his next move.

The man lunged at Ty.

Cassidy spotted a broom that had been left outside by a business owner. She grabbed it. Using it like a javelin, she charged toward the man.

The stick hit him in the gut, and the man fell to the ground, gasping for air.

Ty grabbed him, pulled his arms behind his back, and pulled out some zip ties—which he apparently carried with him. He secured the man's wrists.

One down, but there were two more of these guys still on the loose.

"Go," Ty said, jerking the zip tie tighter. "I've got this one."

Cassidy nodded, hesitating only a minute, before darting toward one of the other men.

This man—a redhead—grabbed a woman who'd been recording the scene on her cell. She screamed in terror, and her phone clattered to the ground.

Cassidy's eyes widened when she saw the man open his mouth and lunge at the woman's neck. Drool escaped from his mouth, beckoning images of a wild and savage caveman.

"Hey!" Cassidy shouted, starting toward him.

The man jerked his head toward her. His wild eyes reminded her of a feral dog in search of food. The drool dripping from his mouth only enhanced the image.

"Get off her." Cassidy drew herself to full height.

Redhead chuckled—long and slow. This man wasn't in his right mind.

Cassidy didn't want to pull her gun out—not with so many civilians around. Not when she was supposed to be undercover. She'd use all her other resources first.

She grabbed the broom again. Using all her momentum, she charged at the man, holding the broom as a shield of sorts as she tackled him to the ground. He hit the cement with a crash. Cassidy landed beside him.

The woman he'd grabbed rolled on her side, and some bystanders rushed to help her.

Cassidy straddled the man on the ground, pinning him in place, while Ty rushed over to help.

Just then, Chief Bozeman and Officer Quinton ran onto the scene. "Go get the other one!" Bozeman shouted.

Quinton took off down the boardwalk.

"What in the world . . . ?" Bozeman muttered, staring at the scene as if it had been a setup for a reality show. He bent down and took the redheaded man from her custody.

"That's a great question," Cassidy said, standing and readjusting her hat. She glanced around and saw the cell cameras recording all of this. What if someone else from DH-7 recognized her from these videos? "Thank goodness for all those CrossFit classes I've taken."

She had to be proactive, to reinforce her cover. Even though danger was closing in, she couldn't blow it now.

"You can say that again." Bozeman jerked the man to his feet, just as Quinton returned, towing the third man behind him. The blond was being guarded by a six-foot-plus man with a long beard and black leather jacket bearing a motorcycle emblem on the side.

It looked as though the situation here was under control.

However, that could have turned out much worse.

———

Cassidy and Ty spent the next hour at the police station giving their statements. The zombie-like men were in lockup, and officers were waiting for the drugs to wear off before questioning them. Cassidy and Ty waited in the lobby for the chief to say they were free to go.

"You sure you're okay?" Ty asked, his gaze going to her forehead. "You have a little cut."

"I'm fine." She stared at the wall across the room, feeling more pensive than she'd like to admit. "Orion has to be behind this. Flakka . . . it's his calling card."

"But we've had the drug on the island before."

"There are different strains of it," she said. "And nothing like this has ever happened here before."

"I've never seen people act so out of their minds," Ty said. "I felt like I'd stepped into a horror flick."

"You and me both."

At that moment, Quinton rushed toward the chief's office, excitement dancing in his eyes. The small building made it easy to overhear conversations—something Cassidy was grateful for at the moment.

"Check this out, boss," Quinton said. "We just found their van. Turns out there's a lot of stolen electronics in the back."

Cassidy and Ty exchanged a glance.

"These are the guys behind the break-ins?" Chief Bozeman asked.

"That's how it appears," Quinton said.

"At least we can close that case." The chief stepped out and turned to them. "Thanks again for your help—

for running toward trouble instead of away. This could have been a lot uglier."

"Any time." Ty paused. "I know you're busy, chief, but could I have a quick word with you?"

Ty was going to mention Orion to him. He and Cassidy had talked about it again and agreed that this was for the best. He would leave out the details about Cassidy's connection to the man.

As Ty disappeared with the chief, Cassidy pulled out her phone and tried to call Serena again. No answer.

Strange. The girl always answered.

A growing sense of worry formed in Cassidy's stomach.

She must have still been frowning when Ty came back out.

"What's wrong?" He paused in front of her, his hands on his hips and his ever-perceptive eyes on hers.

"I haven't been able to catch up with Serena. I've tried her phone several times."

"Maybe she's driving Elsa and can't hear it over the music."

"I don't know. She always answers. And the fact that she wasn't at the ice cream truck earlier bothers me."

"Why don't we go see if we can track her down? I know it will put your mind at ease."

They climbed into Ty's truck and took off down the road. At the parking lot near the boardwalk, they found Elsa still unmanned. Had Serena taken off with a friend and left the truck there? Had she caught a ride back to her car and gone on her merry way?

"Let's check my place and see if her car is still there," Cassidy said. "At least it's something."

Halfway there, her phone rang. Cassidy glanced at the screen, her heart accelerating with hope at the possibility it could be Serena. It was Mac instead.

"I've been at the courthouse. My connections let me in, even though it's a Sunday. Anyway, I've been looking for a marriage license dating back three years ago this week. There are plenty of them, but I haven't found one with any Rich or Richard on it. I just wanted to let you know."

Disappointment bit down. "Thanks for looking. This is pointing to Orion more and more."

"What do you mean?"

Cassidy filled him in on the incident at the boardwalk.

"Be safe, guys." Mac's voice took on a rare seriousness for the cutup. "If it's who you think behind this, I don't like the games he's playing."

"None of us do. I just wanted to keep you updated."

Ty pulled up to her place a few minutes later, and Cassidy's heart lurched. Serena's car still sat in her driveway. She hadn't come back to get it. Cassidy had hoped this was just a display of irresponsibility on the college student's part.

But, like a storm on the horizon, a bad feeling loomed in Cassidy's gut.

Cassidy pulled out her phone and tried calling again.

As expected, there was no answer.

She hit End, shoved the phone back in her pocket, and let out a sigh. "My gut is telling me something is wrong."

"Trust your gut," Ty said.

"Let's go back to the boardwalk. I want to see the truck again. I need to inspect it more closely."

They headed back to Elsa. When they reached her, Cassidy climbed in the driver's seat and glanced around, trying to get insight on Serena's last time in here. Something on the floor beside the front seat caught her eye.

A piece of paper.

Cassidy grabbed it, her hands trembling as the words came into focus.

"I've got your friend," she read. "Do anything rash or tell the police, and she dies. Wait for further instructions . . . Cady Matthews."

TY'S CHEST tightened as he stared at the words. Each was scribbled neatly, purposefully, steadily—all signs of someone who was too comfortable with this situation. His gut churned at that realization. They were dealing with one twisted individual.

"We've got to alert Bozeman," he said.

Cassidy's entire face tightened with anxiety. "I'm not sure that's a great idea. If Orion finds out we involved the police, he'll carry through with his threat. I wish I had more faith in Bozeman's ability to handle something like this correctly, but I don't."

He agreed with her assessment, but they just couldn't stay quiet. "Then we should tell Mac. The three of us together are more capable anyway. We'll find Serena."

Cassidy looked as though her mind was hundreds of miles away. "Orion probably sold the flakka to those guys and set them loose to distract us. This has all been a setup, and I fell for it. How could I have been so stupid?"

Ty's heart lurched as he watched Cassidy, as he saw the struggle inside her. "Hey, come here."

He pulled her toward him and folded her in his arms.

"This is my fault." She stiffened in his embrace, as if she didn't deserve the luxury of being comforted.

"It's not your fault, Cassidy. This is Orion's doing. All of it."

"I knew I shouldn't have gotten close to anyone here. Getting close to people puts them in danger." Cassidy pulled away from him and crossed her arms, constructing an invisible wall.

"Hey, don't go there." Ty reached for her hand, trying to use touch to bring her back to reality. He'd dealt with PTSD before, after being on the battlefield. He suspected that Cassidy was dealing with her own version of it now, and he wanted to help her more than anything. "Pushing me away isn't going to help you right now."

Cassidy squeezed the skin between her eyes. "My duty is to protect people, Ty."

"Protecting other people doesn't mean you have to get yourself killed."

She drew in a few deep breaths. Tugged at the baseball cap she wore. Closed her eyes briefly.

"So what do we do?" She finally snapped from her stupor. "I'm thinking with my emotions here. I need your objectivity."

"Let's drive by Orion's house. See if he's there. If Serena is. I doubt either will be, but we should check."

"Let's go."

They pulled up to Orion's cottage ten minutes later. His SUV was gone, signaling no one was here.

It didn't matter. They'd check it out anyway. Ty parked on the street, and he and Cassidy headed up the steps to the front door.

Cassidy didn't waste any time. She peered in the windows, looking for any sign of Serena.

"Anything?" he asked.

"Nothing."

Ty jiggled the door handle, but it was locked as he'd suspected. He knocked, knowing there would be no answer. He had another way of getting in, though.

"What are you doing?" Cassidy asked, her eyebrows knit together.

"If we break in, Orion is going to turn this back on us. Press charges. Make us appear suspect. I don't want to give him any leverage. I'm calling Wes."

"Why Wes?"

"He has keys to half these rentals. He has to in order to get in and fix things when the owners aren't around." Just as he finished his explanation, Wes answered.

He said he was right down the street, picking up some kayaks. He arrived a few minutes later, his truck pulling a trailer loaded with colorful boats that he'd probably rented out.

Wes took the steps by twos to reach them quickly, a look of concern on his face. "What's going on?"

"We think the person staying here has Serena," Ty said.

Wes's eyes widened. "You think she's here? Why would she be here? What's going on?"

"It's a long story, and we don't have much time," Cassidy said. "But I think that man in town who was looking for me—"

"Your ex?" Wes questioned.

"Yes, him," Cassidy said. "I think he took her."

"Just trust us," Ty said. "Please. We need to get inside. It's life-or-death. I wouldn't have called you otherwise."

Wes hesitated a moment. "You did call the cops, right? This sounds serious."

"This guy threatened us, said that we shouldn't or there would be consequences," Ty said. "In this case, we should listen. I think he's serious about killing Serena if we don't follow his rules."

Wes asked no more questions. He slipped the key in the lock, and the door opened. Without hesitation, Ty and Cassidy rushed inside.

"I'll keep lookout out here," Wes said.

Cassidy rushed the house, her gun drawn as she searched for Serena.

But the place was empty.

They paused in the living room and glanced around. Everything looked so ordinary. There weren't any guns. Any drugs. No incriminating photos even.

It was what he expected—but not what he wanted.

"Let's get out of here," Ty said.

They stepped onto the deck when Ty remembered another question, the one based on his conversation with Jimmy James this morning. "Wes, did you see anyone else here when you worked on his hot tub? A woman, maybe?"

Wes shook his head. "No, it was just him. Sorry."

Ty bit back his disappointment. They'd find answers . . . one way or another.

———

Cassidy and Ty went back to Mac's place to regroup. They'd called him and explained what was going on, and he promised to meet them right away. However, Mac's police scanner indicated a fender bender had stopped traffic near the center of town, so Mac might be a while.

Ty had also called Skye and let her know what happened. She'd insisted on coming over as well. It was only fair to update her—Serena was her niece.

Cassidy couldn't sit still. She paced, trying to organize her thoughts. It didn't matter what Ty had told her. This was entirely her fault. Serena would never have been involved with this if it weren't for Cassidy.

Why was hindsight always 20/20?

Use your mistakes as stepping stones. More Day-at-a-Glance wisdom.

The problem was when Cassidy's mistakes became someone else's heartaches. That wasn't okay.

Someone knocked at the door, pulling Cassidy from

her stupor. Ty answered. Skye stood there. Her face looked pale, her eyes red, and her hands trembled.

She rushed inside, talking at a rapid-fire pace. "What happened? Where's Serena?"

"Someone has her." Ty stood and spoke before Cassidy could. It was probably better that way. "They left a note."

"Is it your ex?" Fire filled her gaze as she turned toward Cassidy.

"I think so. But it's actually—" Cassidy needed to tell the truth, needed to come clean about what was going on.

Before she could finish, Ty jumped in. "That's our best guess. But we don't know anything for sure."

Skye paused and lowered her head, the emotional weight over what had happened tugging at her features. Suddenly, her head snapped up. "We need to call the police."

"He told us not to," Ty said. "We don't think it's a good idea."

"I should be the one to decide that!" Skye said. "She's my niece."

"We know, Skye," Cassidy started, her voice placating and calm. "And it is your decision. We just wouldn't advise it."

"This is your fault." Skye turned to her with wide eyes full of accusation. "This guy followed you here, and now my niece is in danger."

Cassidy's heart pounded with guilt and regret. Hearing it spoken out loud took her remorse to a whole new level. "I know. I'm doing whatever I can to—"

"You should have never come here. Should have never hired Serena."

Ty raised a hand, as if refereeing a fight. "That's not fair, Skye."

Her fire turned toward Ty. "You're only saying that because you've been taken with Cassidy since she stepped foot in town. I knew there was something suspicious about you, Cassidy. Now you've brought trouble with you."

Ty stepped between the women. "Do I need to remind you that Cassidy saved your life? She risked everything to find you earlier this summer."

Skye's face lost a touch of outrage—but not all of it.

"I can't stay around here and chat," Skye finally muttered. "I've got to go find my niece." She turned on her heel and stormed out.

Cassidy closed her eyes. Before she opened them again, she felt Ty's hand on her arm.

"She's upset," he said. "She doesn't mean it. She just has trust issues."

Guilt pounded at Cassidy's temples. "Her words are true, Ty. I shouldn't have come here. I never meant to put anyone in danger."

"She'll come to her senses," Ty said. "Give her time."

"I deserve every bit of her anger." Cassidy paced toward the door. "And more."

Ty stayed where he was, watching her with that

observant expression. "That's not true. You're one of the most selfless people I know, Cassidy. I couldn't let you tell Skye the truth. I know it's tempting you."

She had almost told her. She didn't even care if she was a target anymore. She just wanted Serena to be safe.

Images of DH-7's victims replayed in her head, like a bad TV special. Each one made her shudder. "It doesn't seem fair to keep her in the dark."

"The more people who know, the more danger that will flood this way," Ty murmured. "We don't want more DH-7 members showing up here."

Cassidy didn't bother arguing, even though she wanted to. Besides, Ty was right. Once her emotions cleared, she would see that. Until then, she'd trust his instincts.

CHAPTER
EIGHTEEN

A MOMENT LATER, Cassidy's phone buzzed. She straightened as she looked at the screen. A picture popped up.

"Ty, it's Serena." She clicked on it, just as Ty came to stand beside her.

She drew in a quick breath when she saw the image.

It was Serena, all right. Except she was no longer the idealistic college student with hopeful, bright eyes. No, she looked scared. Terrified.

A white gag covered her mouth. Dirt—or was that a bruise—was smudged around one eye. Her hair was in a misshapen ponytail.

Cassidy soaked in the background, trying to discern some detail that might give her a clue as to where to find Serena. But it was just a white wall. No shadows or anything else distinguishable about it.

The words at the bottom of the screen came into focus.

Instructions coming soon.

She closed her eyes. The only way Orion could have gotten this number was if Serena gave it to him. What was he doing to the girl? Had he hurt her? Because Cassidy would make him pay if he had.

Carefully, she typed her reply.

Let Serena go.

Cassidy waited, the seconds feeling like hours. Finally, Orion responded.

We do this on my terms.

That sounded exactly like the Orion she knew. Arrogant. Heartless. Controlling.

Serena has nothing to do with this. It's between you and me.

You ruined my friend's life. Now I'm going to ruin yours. And theirs.

Cassidy's breath caught. What did that even mean? She knew. She just couldn't mentally go there right now.

"Don't do this," she typed back.

"Too late. Already done. In memory of Raul Sanders —the man you murdered. Adios."

Cassidy's heart thudded in her chest as she turned to Ty. "We need to try and track Serena's phone. I know it probably won't help, but we've got to try."

Ty's jaw looked stiff as he stared at Cassidy's phone. "Let's get on it."

———

While Mac met with an old friend to see if he could ping Serena's phone, Ty and Cassidy headed to the ferry. She couldn't stay at Mac's any longer. She had to take action.

"We need to see if anyone there has seen Orion. It's the only way off the island," Cassidy said.

"He could have taken a small boat," Ty said, gripping the steering wheel.

"He wouldn't have done that. He hates water—he can't swim." He'd told her that once when they'd gone to a house with a pool. He wouldn't get anywhere near it. When other people began throwing each other in the water, a sweat actually broke out across his forehead.

Ty glanced at her. "A ferry is still a boat."

"But it's large enough that it wouldn't freak him out as much. If he left, he took the ferry. I'm sure of it."

"Let's see what the attendants say," Ty said.

They parked at the terminal and made their way to the workers at the gates. Cassidy had pulled up both Orion and Serena's pictures on her phone, and she showed them to the attendants.

"He doesn't look familiar," one of the men said.

"Do you have video footage?" Ty asked. "This guy drives a white SUV."

The attendant shrugged. "There are a surprising number of people who drive that kind of vehicle. Popular color."

"Please, this is important," Cassidy said. "We need to see the video."

The man sighed. "Go talk to Willard in the office. Maybe he can help you."

"Thank you," Cassidy said. "And how many trips have already left today?"

"Six."

Six. She could probably rule out the first two or three since she could account for Serena up until around one o'clock. But that still left three other departures. Each ferry could hold around three dozen cars. Locals and businesses had their own priority lane, which would narrow that number even more.

Cassidy marched up to the man in the office, whose nameplate proudly proclaimed he was Willard, and explained that she was looking for someone who might be in danger.

He barely flinched. "We need a warrant."

"Please, this is urgent," Ty said.

Willard shifted, seeming to take Ty more seriously. Typical. "Did you tell the police?"

"We can't," Cassidy said. "Not if we want her to stay alive."

Willard sighed. "Don't tell anyone I did this, okay?"

"Thank you." Relief washed through Cassidy. Some progress was still progress.

The man found the footage on his computer and stood from his desk. "I'm taking a bathroom break. You have ten minutes. And if anyone asks, I didn't know what you two were doing."

They sat behind his desk and began scrolling through the video, which was surprisingly clear. Several cars looked similar, but none fit the description of Orion's.

"If he's not on that ferry, he's on the island still," Cassidy said. "That's the good news."

"So we just need to find him," Ty said.

"That's right. But we need someone to guard the ferry terminal, just in case he decides to leave."

"Let me call Austin—and then you and I can keep looking."

————

With Austin camped out at the terminal, Cassidy had already determined her next step.

"We need to go to the police station," she said.

"I thought you weren't going to tell the chief," Ty said.

"I'm not. But I need to talk to those guys who took that flakka," she said. "Maybe they have an idea of where Orion is hiding out."

"What are you going to tell the chief?" Ty took off down the road.

"I'm not sure yet. But I'll think of something."

They pulled up a few minutes later, and Cassidy stormed inside the station. She bypassed the receptionist and went straight to the chief's office. He startled when he saw her and then stood.

"Ms. Livingston . . . Ty . . . how can I help you two?" He wiped some crumbs from his shirt and straightened.

"I need to talk to those guys," Cassidy said.

"The zombie guys?" He chuckled, as if he found her request funny. "Why would you want to do that?"

"I think they vandalized Elsa," she said, hoping her cover story worked. "I need to know the truth."

The chief's humor seemed to disappear. "I'm sorry to hear that, but we don't let civilians interrogate suspects."

"I know. But can you make an exception, Chief? Please."

He swallowed hard, indecision evident in his gaze. "You're asking a lot—especially for a simple ice cream truck."

Cassidy softened her voice. "Please, Chief. I helped you catch these guys. All I ask is that, in return, you give me a few minutes alone with them. I assume they're out of their drug stupor now."

"They are. And they look miserable. Hungover, almost."

"Perfect. No better time to talk to them." They hadn't returned to their full senses yet.

The chief sighed and ran a hand over his pasty face. "I don't like breaking the rules."

"Then don't break them," Ty said. "Just give us a few minutes with them. It won't cause any harm. In fact, no one has to know but us."

The chief eyeballed Cassidy. She was on the verge of blowing her cover. She knew she was. But this was important. Cassidy had to find Serena.

Finally, Bozeman nodded. "Fine. But I'm not going to make a habit of this."

"I wouldn't expect it." Cassidy tried to convey her gratitude with her voice.

"Follow me."

They walked down a small hallway toward the holding cell. The men sat inside the room, its only occupants.

"Have at it," the chief said. "You've got five minutes."

The guys didn't pay Cassidy and Ty much attention. In fact, they didn't even seem to recognize them. That was what drugs could do to a person. They were a huge mistake and an increasing problem.

One of the men stood, while the others continued to look like they'd nearly collapsed on a bench.

The one standing must be the leader of the bunch. As a general rule, the first one to speak was.

Cassidy grabbed one of the bars and leaned toward them. "Hey."

The redhead glanced up, but his eyes were dull and his gaze distant.

"Come here," she said.

Ty stood in the background, ready to jump in if necessary. She was so thankful he was comfortable enough in his manhood to let her take the lead.

"Who are you?" the guy muttered. His eyes were bloodshot, his skin pasty, and his white shirt stained with sweat.

"It's not important. I have a question for you."

His tired gaze flickered to hers. "Why should I answer it?"

"Because otherwise I'm going to press charges against you for this." Cassidy turned to show him the scratch on her temple and elbow—injuries he'd inflicted.

He scowled and let out an irritated groan. "What do you want to know?"

Cassidy held up her phone and showed him a picture of Orion. "Is this the guy you got the drugs from?"

He glanced at the photo and shrugged. "Maybe."

"Is it or isn't it?" Ty stepped closer, all bristly and Navy SEAL tough. "Answer the lady's question."

The man flinched and seemed to sober even more. "Yeah, that looks like him. Except different. He looks . . . how do you say it? More . . . refined now."

"How'd you meet him?" Cassidy asked.

Redhead shrugged and raked a hand through his thick, wiry hair. "He approached my friends and me. We were surfing. Said he knew what we were doing."

"What were you doing?" Cassidy asked.

He lowered his head and sighed, as if every part of the conversation felt painful and exhausting. "Stealing."

"So you could buy drugs," Ty finished.

"Yeah, so we could buy drugs." His low, listless tone signaled defeat. "He said he had a great new drug we could try. Our first hit was on him."

How convenient, Cassidy mused. "Where did you meet him to get the drugs?"

"At the beach. Joyner's Point."

"Joyner's Point?" Cassidy wasn't familiar with it.

"It's a surfer's beach," Ty explained. "It's pretty secluded from tourists, and the shore break there is perfect for catching waves."

At least they were getting somewhere.

She glanced back at his two friends, just as one of them rolled from the wall-mounted bench onto the floor —and didn't even wake up. Yeah, doing drugs was really living the life, she thought sarcastically. Who wouldn't want this?

"When was the last time you saw this guy?" Cassidy asked.

"This morning. He gave us the drugs around lunchtime. Told us to go ride the Ferris wheel after we took them for an experience we'd never forget. Taking the drugs was the last thing I remember, though."

The Ferris wheel hadn't been far from the restaurant where Ty and Cassidy had lunch.

"I take it you didn't make it to the Ferris wheel?" Ty asked.

"I don't think so."

"Is there anything else you can tell us about this guy?" Cassidy asked. "We need to find him."

"Not really. He said he had some business to take care of so he probably wouldn't be seeing us again. But he was trying to make some connections, so the drug would be readily available if we wanted more."

"But no more details?" Ty asked.

"Only one other thing. He kept talking about his wife. So much so that it was weird. Like he was doing it on purpose."

Cassidy's mind whirled. "Did he say what her name was?"

"Yeah, it was Alisha."

———

"So, Alisha was his girlfriend? Ty asked as they climbed into his truck.

Cassidy nodded. "Yes. She betrayed him, so he murdered her. I'm sure that was Orion's way of sending me a message, Ty. He wanted me to know that no one betrays him."

He tamped down the surge of anger that rose in him. Anger wouldn't get him anywhere right now. No, he had to keep a cool head.

He'd seen a different side of Cassidy over the past couple hours. The tough, assertive side. He could imagine her as a detective, interrogating suspects.

It was impressive, to say the least, and gave him a

whole new level of respect for her. It also reminded him yet again that her life wasn't here and she was meant for bigger things. His gut twisted at the reminder, at the uncertainty regarding their future.

"How about we go check on Austin?"

"Sure," Cassidy said. "And then I'd like to search the island for Orion's SUV. I know it's a long shot. And we need to check in with Mac."

It sounded like a long process—but if they found Serena, it would be worth it. "Let's go."

They pulled up to the ferry. Austin's truck sat near the loading dock. They parked and made their way toward it. When Austin rolled down his window, Ty spotted Skye in the car with him. He wondered if she'd calmed down yet.

He understood her frustration, but she didn't need to take it out on Cassidy.

He glanced at Skye now, but she raised her chin and turned her head away. She was still mad, but hopefully with some time she'd be okay.

He prayed that was the case, and he prayed for her comfort right now. Having someone you loved disappear at the hands of a madman couldn't be easy. He thought about his mom and all she'd gone through with her cancer.

No, the suffering of loved ones was beyond not easy —it could be devastating.

Ty's gaze flickered back to Austin. "Anything?"

He shook his head and took another sip of his

energy drink. "No, nothing. I thought I might have seen the vehicle, but it was a family of five inside. Sorry, man. Any updates on your end?"

"No, but we're working on it. We found out Orion sold a few local teens some drugs. We don't think he's left the island, so we're going to continue looking. We haven't given up yet."

"Keep us updated," Austin said. "We'll stay here, just to make sure he doesn't try to leave. I did wonder if he might have gotten a different vehicle. I've been searching faces. Even got out a few times and walked between the cars. Told people I lost my dog."

"Good move," Ty said. "And good point. I'll ask the chief if any stolen cars have been reported."

Just as Cassidy and Ty climbed back into his truck, Mac called. Cassidy put her phone on speaker.

"Did you find anything?" she asked.

"The cell pinged here on the island two hours ago. It must be off right now because we're getting nothing."

"That confirms what we've learned also," Cassidy said. "We believe they're still here on Lantern Beach."

"I'm going to use some more of my connections to see if I can watch some street cams in the area. Maybe we can follow their movement that way."

"That would be great," Cassidy said. She asked him to look into any stolen vehicles, and he agreed. "We're going to drive all over the island and look for Orion's SUV. I know he may have ditched it. But, whatever he did, I want to figure it out."

"Okay, let's connect later."

She hung up and turned to Ty. "As far as I'm concerned, he's trapped here. We've got to find him."

He squeezed her hand. "We will. Let's just keep working."

THE NIGHTTIME AIR was heavy around Cady, dampness from an earlier rain shower still hanging in the air. Down the street, a dog barked. Didn't just bark —it snarled, and the sound of it jumping against a chain-link fence caused another shiver to run down her spine.

Somewhere in the distance, a car revved its engine before charging down the road.

This was not the kind of neighborhood a single gal wanted to get lost in. Some communities aged well and with character. Others seemed to age, but the process invited in less-than-savory folks who wanted cheap places to hide.

"You ready for this?" Orion's eyes reminded Cady of a snake seconds from striking its unsuspecting prey.

"Of course." Cady pushed down her rush of nerves and tried to quell the panic that threatened to claim her muscles and thoughts.

She couldn't kill someone. Yet, if she didn't, she'd be a dead woman, and all of this would be for nothing.

"I want you to do it," Orion said, falling in step beside her.

She glanced up and saw his gaze still held challenge, a promise that if she didn't pull through, there would be deadly consequences.

"I'd be honored." Cady's pulse spiked so high she felt lightheaded. She had to keep up the act, to sound tough and street smart and loyal. But, internally, she rebelled against all of this.

"Let's figure out where Reginald is before we announce ourselves," Orion said. "You take the front of the house, I'll take the back."

"It's a plan." She gripped her gun, thankful to be out of Orion's sight for a moment. The last thing she needed was for him to watch her every move.

As soon as he disappeared around the corner, Cady checked her gun's magazine. It was loaded, just like she'd left it. But maybe she could work this in her favor. It would be a long shot, but her makeshift plan just might work.

She drew in a deep breath as she shoved the magazine back in place. She could do this.

But she didn't want to. Every fiber of her being wanted to escape and forget about this assignment.

What kind of detective was she? She should be brave. Tough. At the moment, she felt anything but.

Cady climbed onto the rickety porch. Several folding lawn chairs cluttered the space, along with some old milk crates topped with ashtrays. One of the boards beneath her black boot nearly gave way.

The shoes were part of her look. Skin-tight jeans. A form-fitting T-shirt. Black leather jacket. Stark black hair, heavy eye makeup.

But changing her appearance hadn't changed who she was inside. Cady Matthews was still the girl desperate to prove herself, who wanted to belong, who struggled to find her place in the world. The poor little rich girl who had everything yet nothing of importance.

She pressed herself against the dingy shingle siding of the house and peered into the window. Through the thin, striped curtains, she could make out the form of someone sitting on the couch inside.

Reginald.

She'd halfway been hoping he wouldn't be here.

She swallowed hard. What if she told Orion he wasn't here and—

Just as the thought entered her mind, Orion appeared around the corner. "He must be at the front of the house. His car is here so he should be too."

Cady nodded stiffly. "That's him on the couch."

"Good. I'll get the door and do the talking. But you're pulling the trigger. Go for his heart. We need to get in and get out. As soon as people hear gunfire, the police will come."

"Isn't this too easy?" Cady asked. "Maybe we should grab him and draw this out."

That was DH-7's usual MO, and maybe it would buy her some time.

A gleam filled Orion's gaze. "That's the way we usually prefer to do things. But this one is a hit-and-run."

Probably because he wanted to test Cady's loyalty. Why else would he change the way he operated?

"Whatever you say, Const," she said. A quiver found its way into her voice, but she caught it before the tell claimed each word.

On the count of three, Orion kicked the door open and rushed into the house.

Cady followed behind, gripping her gun as sweat covered her entire body.

This had to work.

Please let it work.

Lord, I don't know if You're real or not. I know Lucy loved You, though. I could really use Your favor right now for this plan to succeed.

When Cady admitted it, she understood the emptiness inside members of DH-7. She had a different kind of emptiness.

And she was tired of it. She needed a change. But how? And was it even possible while she was deep undercover?

This wasn't the time to think about it.

Reginald jumped off the couch, his bowl of popcorn spilling across the floor. He raised his hands in the air, his sport jersey jerking up and exposing his broad belly.

"What are you doing here?" The man's eyes were wide with fear and realization. He knew exactly why they were here and what was about to happen.

"We know you betrayed us." Orion's voice came out with a deep, bitter growl.

"Naw, man. I'd never do that." But even Reginald didn't sound convinced—only desperate.

"You shared our secrets with the Blood Brotherhood," Orion continued.

"I wouldn't do that." Reginald swung his head back and forth, a pleading whine tugging at the words. "You know me better than that."

"Stop arguing!" Orion shouted. "We know it's true. And you know what happens to people who betray us."

"Let's talk this through, man," Reginald said, his breathing labored and shallow. "I can explain. You don't understand."

"It's too late for that." Orion nodded at Cady. "My friend here is going to show you what happens to snitches like you."

Cady raised her gun. Without hesitating, she pulled the trigger.

The bullet hit him squarely in the chest—just like Orion had instructed.

Reginald gripped his heart and fell onto the couch, letting out a final moan before landing face-down on the floor.

Cady's own heart pounded wildly in her chest. What had she done? What if her plan hadn't worked?

"I underestimated you." Orion glanced at her, humor dancing in his gaze. "Didn't think you'd do it."

"Of course I would." She shoved her gun back into

her waistband, giving off a nonchalant air that defined this culture.

"Alright, let's get out of here before the cops show up." He nodded toward the door.

"Let me just make sure he's really dead first," Cady said. "Maybe get a picture to prove it."

"Good idea."

She rushed toward Reginald. Put her finger at his neck. Waited to feel for a pulse.

"He's dead," she muttered, snapping a quick photo with her phone. "Let's go."

Before Cady could hurry out the door, Orion grabbed her arm and stopped her with a harsh jerk.

Her heart pounded harder.

He was onto her, wasn't he? This was the moment where everything came to a head—came to a violent end.

Instead, Orion pressed his lips into hers.

Repulsion filled Cady's stomach at the feel of his mouth against hers.

Finally, he stepped back, just as abruptly as he'd stepped forward.

"What was that for?" She resisted the urge to gag or wipe the feel of him from her mouth.

Cady knew what it was about. Not romance or relationship. No, it was about domination.

Another wave of nausea rushed through her.

"You're a mystery," he muttered.

The rancid breath that hit her face was so toxic she could hardly breathe.

He continued, "But you just proved yourself loyal. Now let's go."

Just before Cady stepped out the door, she glanced back at Reginald.

He stirred, ever so slightly.

Cady's heart slowed.

Her plan had worked.

At the first opportunity, she'd get in touch with Samuel. Let him know that Reginald would be a great informant. Send his photo.

She'd used a rubber bullet on the man. He'd have an awful and painful bruise, but he should be okay. The force of the blast had knocked him out just long enough for her plan to work.

If the police could grab Reginald, they could help him fake his death. He would be valuable to the task force. If he didn't cooperate, then DH-7 would finish him.

And they'd finish Cady also.

It had been risky, but she hoped the risk would pay off.

In fact, she'd bet everything on it.

CHAPTER
TWENTY

TODAY'S GOALS: FIND SERENA.
MAKE ORION PAY.

CASSIDY AND TY spent the entire night searching the island for Orion's SUV. They didn't find it. If he was still in Lantern Beach, he was well hidden. They'd gone down every street multiple times.

They returned to Mac's place after grabbing a quick breakfast. Cassidy didn't have an appetite, but Ty had insisted she eat something. She'd nibbled a sausage and egg biscuit from the General Store—though she didn't taste a bite. All she really wanted to do was formulate a new plan. The ferry hadn't provided any leads, nor had the search for Orion's vehicle.

They'd no sooner greeted Kujo when Cassidy's phone buzzed.

"It's him." Her pulse spiked as she looked at her screen. "Orion."

Ty and Mac gathered around her.

"It says, 'Get on the 9:00 ferry. Further instructions

coming.'" Cassidy glanced at her watch. It was 8:30 now. "We'll barely make it."

"Let's go." Ty grabbed his keys and started toward the door.

Mac grabbed his gun from the table where he'd left it. "I'm coming too. You'll need all the backup you can get."

Cassidy wasn't going to argue. They hopped in Ty's truck and took off toward the ferry terminal. They couldn't miss this departure.

But as soon as they pulled up, a flashing sign over the entrance to the loading area signaled a setback.

"The ferry's full," Cassidy muttered.

"Let's see if we can find another way," Ty said. "Maybe they'll take walk-ons."

Ty parked, and they darted from the truck. They all reached the boat just as the gates were coming down. The same attendant from yesterday was standing at the entrance ramp.

"I know it's too late to drive on, but we've got to get on this ferry," Cassidy said. "It's an emergency."

The attendant stared at them. "Medical?"

Mac stepped up and pulled the toothpick from his mouth. "Remember that time I let you go after you got into that fight outside of Shorty's?"

His cheeks reddened. "I do."

"Your momma would have killed you," Mac continued.

"I know."

"You owe me one, and this is important. We wouldn't ask this otherwise."

"We usually don't take walk-ons." His gaze darted around, as if looking for anyone who might be listening.

"Please, make an exception," Cassidy said. "Just this once."

He tugged his collar and glanced around again. "I guess this one time. Just don't make me lose my job."

"We won't," Cassidy said.

"And I'll keep your secret," Mac said.

The three of them rushed onto the ferry with only seconds to spare. The boat lurched as it started its journey across the water to Ocracoke. They wove their way between cars to the railing.

Cassidy glanced around, soaking in the cars loaded with kayaks and boogie boards and beach chairs. Looked at the faces of children as they peered out the windows. Watched the seagulls as they circled the boat looking for stray food.

"Do you think she's on here?" Cassidy asked.

"Why else would he want you to come?" Mac asked.

"I don't know. I don't understand his game." Cassidy glanced around again. Where did she even begin? "Is there a lobby?"

Ty nodded. "Yeah, you can buy snacks and sit down there if you don't want to wait in your car. There's also an observation deck above that, some bathrooms, and the crew's quarters. I've spent a lot of time on these boats."

"Why don't we split up and see if we can find Orion or Serena?" Cassidy added before Ty or Mac could argue, "I'll be okay. I have my gun."

They both hesitated a moment before nodding.

"Be careful," Ty said.

"You too," she said. "Meet back here in twenty minutes, okay?"

Cassidy took the lobby area. She entered it quickly but paused. There was no need to alarm people by acting frantic. Instead, she took a deep breath and scanned the place.

There was no sign of either Orion or Serena. Not from her initial perusal, at least.

But what had she expected? That they'd be sitting at a table having coffee together like old friends?

Orion's SUV wasn't on this boat. If they were here, Orion had either gotten a different car or he'd gotten on a different way.

The trip to Ocracoke should take an hour and a half. Thirty minutes had already passed, and there were no updates.

She met Mac and Ty again outside by the railing. They hadn't seen anything either. She drew in a deep breath, trying to keep her composure. But as she soaked in the life around her, urgency pressed in on her.

Kids squealed as they spotted dolphins in the water. An elderly couple stood close to each other, the nostalgic look in their eyes hinting of fond memories. A family argued about where to eat lunch.

Innocent lives . . . they surrounded her.

Just what was Orion planning?

"Maybe this was an excuse to get us off the island, so he could do something else devious," Cassidy said.

As soon as the words left her lips, her phone buzzed. She quickly glanced at the screen.

"Good job following directions," she read aloud. "I thought you should know that I've left a bomb onboard. Happy hunting."

———

"A bomb?" Ty felt the air leave his lungs at the gravity of the situation. "We've got to get people off this ferry."

"I'll go tell the captain what's going on," Mac said, already springing toward the crew.

"I'll start looking for the bomb." Cassidy's voice sounded tight enough to break.

"I'll take upstairs," Ty said.

They rushed in their separate directions. Ty tore up the stairs, dodging passengers who eyed him with confused expressions.

This guy could be bluffing—but they couldn't take that chance, not when innocent lives were on the line.

He scanned everything as he passed it. The stairs. The roofline. The deck below.

Nothing yet.

He rushed inside the cabin area. More travelers gave him strange looks, like he'd lost his mind or like he was a terrorist. Fear lingered in their eyes.

Ty surveyed the area. Probably twenty people were

up here—families mostly. There were also a few tables, a fire extinguisher, and cloudy windows.

He looked under every table, in every corner, but there was nothing.

When he was sure there was no bomb in the area, he went back downstairs. Cassidy found him. She looked breathless, and adrenaline seemed to lace each of her quick, reflexive actions.

"Anything?" Cassidy pulled her sunglasses down and stared him in the eye.

Ty shook his head, wishing he had different news. "No, you?"

"I didn't see anything suspicious either," she said. "Mac is searching the crew's cabin. I'm not sure they're taking this as seriously as we'd like."

"Let's keep looking. Maybe we missed something."

"I'll take the upstairs this time."

He wove between the cars, searching the edges of the boat. There were ropes. A fire extinguisher. Some life jackets shoved into cubbies.

Nothing that looked like a bomb.

As he started back, something caught his eye.

A box in the back of a truck had something unusual sticking out from one of its edges.

Ty paused and sucked in a breath. Knockoff purses.

Slowly, carefully, he pulled back the cardboard top and moved the handbags out of the way.

What he saw inside stole his breath.

It was a bomb, all right.

And the countdown had already started. They only had ten minutes to defuse it before this whole boat became a part of the Graveyard of the Atlantic.

CHAPTER
TWENTY-ONE

CASSIDY STARED AT THE DEVICE—THE wires, the battery, a vat of liquid—some kind of flammable substance—and a cell phone attached to it all to act as the switch.

She'd taken classes on explosives, but she'd never defused a live one, so she was obviously not an expert.

"Mac, you were just brushing up on your bomb-defusing skills, right?" Cassidy asked. "Ty, did you deal with this as a SEAL?"

"I have." Mac knelt beside it, and Ty joined him, along with the boat's captain.

The men stared at it a few seconds, as if cataloging all the information on the wiring and type of bomb. The rest of the crew seemed as stunned as Cassidy. But they didn't have the luxury of wallowing in it.

"Everyone, move to the other side of the boat," Cassidy yelled.

"We need everyone to put on a life vest," one crew member said.

Another attendant got on a radio. But it was too late to turn back. They wouldn't make it in time.

It was either defuse this bomb or this ferry was going to explode, sending everyone onboard into the water. The amount of shrapnel and the vehicles being propelled in the blast would kill almost everyone.

Cassidy could hardly stomach the thought.

"This isn't like any bomb I've seen before," Mac said.

"One wrong move and we're all gone," Ty reminded him.

"That's exactly what I'm afraid of."

Cassidy glanced at the digital timer.

"We have less than a minute," Cassidy told them. The realization took her breath away. "And we're too far away from land to evacuate. We're running out of time, guys."

"Tell everyone to hold on," Ty shouted. "It's too late for lifeboats."

Thirty-five.

Cassidy didn't ask questions. Instead, she turned around and shouted directions. But in her mind, she could still see that timer. She mentally counted down the seconds.

Twenty-five.

She knew they didn't have much time. What was Ty's plan?

She glanced back over at him and saw him grab the bomb.

"Everybody, get down!" he yelled.

Fifteen.

In one swift motion, he pulled his arm back and launched the device into the inlet.

Only seconds after it hit the water, an explosion ripped through the air. Water sprayed high. The boat jerked to the side, rocking with the blast. People screamed.

After what seemed like an eternity—but in reality, probably only ten seconds—the ferry righted itself. The water stopped spraying. And everyone seemed to take a breath together.

Cassidy paused and glanced around, taking inventory of everyone in sight.

They were okay, she realized.

Everyone was okay.

She released her breath.

That could have turned out much worse. Much, much worse.

She exchanged a glance with Ty and Mac. Their gazes said it all.

Relief. Exhaustion. Gratitude.

That had been way too close.

———

Law enforcement swarmed the ferry docks. Everyone had been called in—the Lantern Beach PD, the Coast

Guard, the state police, the NCSBI. Probably others, as well.

All of the passengers had been relegated to the parking lot—once it had been cleared and a police line had been set up. Paramedics treated a few people for whiplash or minor cuts.

Mac, Ty, and Cassidy had been pulled aside—asked to stand near the building that housed management offices. The position allowed them to observe all the activity.

Cassidy watched as they questioned the truck driver. She stood just close enough that she could hear.

"I didn't put that box in my truck," he said. "I have no idea where it came from."

The man looked to be in his seventies, and his voice sounded as frail and shaky as he looked.

She believed the man. The truck driver wasn't behind this. No, somehow Orion had planted that box in his vehicle.

Could this tie in with Jimmy James? It had been a box of knockoff purses. Cassidy wasn't sure yet. But everything was a possibility at this point.

"I stopped at the General Store and got some gas," the truck driver continued. "I didn't bother to look in the back of my truck. I have some salvage metal back there that I was taking in to be recycled. Didn't think anything of it."

Cassidy's anxiety climbed. She knew her turn was coming. The police would question her. And she knew she'd blow her cover if she told the police the complete truth. She had to keep perspective here, despite the tug–of-war inside her.

"Let me take the lead," Ty whispered.

Relief salved her heart at his offer. The last thing she wanted was to get him in trouble, but . . . it was worth a try. "Are you sure?"

He nodded without a touch of hesitancy. "I'm sure."

Just as the words left his mouth, a man approached them. "I'm Detective Dan Peterson with the North Carolina State Bureau of Investigation. I'm the lead on this case for now. Can I have a word with all of you?"

"Of course," Ty said.

Ty kept a hand on Cassidy's back as Peterson led them away from any listening ears.

"Can you tell me your version of what happened?" he started.

Cassidy let Ty and Mac talk. Ty, the ex-navy SEAL. Mac, the former police chief. It made sense that they had known what to do. She hoped she simply looked like Ty's girlfriend, the woman who'd helped but who'd otherwise been clueless.

However, Peterson had gotten her name. Her fake social. Her address.

Samuel had set those things up for her, so hopefully, they'd fly if the police ran a check on her. But the situation was precarious at best and left her feeling unsettled.

"Why did you think there was a bomb in the first place?" the investigator asked.

"Because I got this text earlier." Ty had Cassidy's phone already in his pocket, and he held up the text.

Peterson studied the screen. "Someone randomly texted you this?"

Ty nodded. "I believe it came from a man who confronted me in the parking lot at church yesterday."

He looked unconvinced. "So someone randomly confronted you? Then texted you?"

Ty raked a hand through his hair. He wasn't as nervous as he let on. No, he was testing out his acting chops as well, if Cassidy had to guess.

"Someone broke into my girlfriend's cottage earlier, and we've been on the lookout," Ty said. "I believe her ex-boyfriend may be indirectly involved."

"What does that mean?" Peterson asked.

"We think he was selling drugs to the guys who did this," Ty said.

"I can verify everything he's said." Mac nodded confidentially. "We've been looking into it for our own peace of mind. We must have pushed too hard."

"Why would this man put so many people at risk just to avoid potentially getting caught for some drugs? As far as I've heard, he wasn't even on the police's radar." Peterson's gaze traveled to each of them as he waited for an answer that would appease him.

"I believe he's a twisted individual who likes to play games," Ty said.

"He would have to be to do something like this." Detective Peterson frowned. "Could this tie in with your time as a SEAL?"

Ty shook his head. "I don't believe that's the case."

Mac shifted. "Anything else?"

Peterson glanced up, his gaze heavy. Uncertain. Calculating. Finally, he shook his head. "Not at this time. But if anything comes up, we'll be calling. Stay close."

"We will," Ty said.

Cassidy released her breath. That was over. For now. However, all of this was far from being finished.

———

As soon as they got back to the truck, Ty handed Cassidy her phone. "It buzzed again while I was talking to the investigator."

She took it from him, climbed in, and read the first message aloud for Ty and Mac to hear.

> You passed the first test. Let it be a sign. The clock is ticking and the water's rising.

Cassidy shook her head and glanced back and forth from Mac to Ty. "What does that even mean?"

"It's just like you said," Ty muttered. "He's playing games with you."

"Games that could have killed dozens of people, including innocent children. I knew he was sick and twisted, but I didn't realize the extent. What if that means there's some kind of clock ticking before Serena dies?"

A shadow crossed Ty's face at her words. "We need to go talk to Jimmy James. Maybe he'll have some answers."

"I agree. That bomb was found in a box of his purses."

They headed toward the marina. As soon as they got there, Ty and Cassidy started to climb out. Mac lingered behind.

"I'm going to stay here in the truck," he said. "Something about that bomb is bothering me. It's just a hunch, but I need to check into a few things."

Cassidy and Ty headed down the dock, searching for Jimmy James. Halfway across the marina, they spotted him on a pier in the distance, unloading more cargo from a boat. He looked up. As soon as he recognized them, he froze.

In the next instant, he sprinted away.

"You've got to be kidding me," Ty muttered, taking off after him.

Cassidy followed behind, desperate not to let the man get away.

As Jimmy James reached the end of the pier, Cassidy realized he'd hit a dead end. Tempest water crashed against the pilings there, screaming of danger.

Just as Cassidy slowed her steps, Jimmy James looked back at them. Then he jumped into the water.

TWENTY-TWO

TY DOVE into the water after Jimmy James. If running was a sign of guilt, then Jimmy James was the poster child right now.

Cassidy watched from the edge of the pier, ready to help however necessary. She'd be more use up here, however. She watched as Ty easily caught up to Jimmy James in the water.

A Navy SEAL versus a dockworker? The SEAL definitely had the upper hand.

Jimmy James struggled against Ty's grip. Water flew into the air. Grunts sounded.

Cassidy reached for her gun and then glanced at the crowd around her.

Was Orion here?

She didn't see him. But she needed to be prepared, just in case things turned south quickly.

Finally, Ty put the man in a headlock and began dragging him back to shore.

A few other men helped pull Jimmy James and Ty back onto the pier. Jimmy James sputtered on the weathered wood, his breathing labored.

Ty rose to full height and shook off the water, unaffected by the plunge, except for his shoulder, Cassidy noted. He rolled it back and cringed. Hopefully, he hadn't undone what surgery had repaired.

"We've got this from here," Ty told the crowd. "Thanks for your help."

Ty and Cassidy stood over Jimmy James, daring him to make another impulsive move. He raised his hands in the air as he stood, signaling defeat. "Look, I'm sorry."

"Did you really think running was the best option?" Ty glared at him. This was more than a suspect on the run. Ty had invested in this man. He'd believed in him. Offered him the benefit of the doubt. And now this.

"I freaked out." He belted the words out in short syllables that made him sound like his nose was plugged.

"Why'd you run?" Ty demanded.

He gasped in another breath, his bloodshot eyes as grotesque as a dead fish—only in a different way. "I figured you learned the truth."

"And what truth is that?"

"That guy stopped me in the church parking lot as I was leaving," he started.

Cassidy's blood went a little colder. Orion. At church. On purpose. All of this had been on purpose.

"And what did he say?" Ty continued. The hard set

of his jaw amplified his experience level. He'd questioned terrorists.

He could handle Jimmy James. Cassidy's heart fluttered with admiration.

"He told me he'd heard about my handbag business."

Cassidy shifted to see Jimmy James's eyes more clearly, to ascertain whether or not he was telling the truth. "How did he hear about that business?"

As far as Cassidy knew, those purses were hush-hush. Why else the secrecy at the lighthouse?

"He seemed to have connections, and I didn't ask questions," Jimmy James said. "Anyway, he offered to pay me double what I usually get. He said it was urgent that he have the bags and that he have them as soon as possible."

"Weren't you afraid of angering your other clients?" Ty asked.

"Of course. But I'll get more in and make them happy. This guy said he was only in town for a short time. I needed the money. Rent is coming due, and my roommate just moved out."

"And you didn't think this urgency odd?" Ty asked. "Even though someone had been asking about Cassidy earlier?"

His face reddened. "He seemed nice enough. I figured it was just a misunderstanding."

Ty let out a long, unhindered sigh before shaking his head. "So you sold him the purses. Did you have them with you?"

"As a matter of fact I did."

"And then what?" Ty asked.

Jimmy James swallowed hard and looked off at the marina a moment. His face reddened again. The tough guy was finding all of this a bit embarrassing.

Good. He should be.

"Then his girlfriend took them, put them in her car, and he apparently went to church," he finished.

"Wait . . . what girlfriend?" His words caused Cassidy to flinch with surprise.

"I told you I saw him with a woman." His voice held a hurt tone, like he was offended they hadn't been listening earlier.

"She was with him again yesterday?" Cassidy clarified.

"Yeah, right beside him."

The woman hadn't gone to church with him. Why? Who was she? "What did she look like?"

"She was pretty, I guess. Long, dark hair." He shrugged. "I don't know. He wasn't the type of guy I wanted to catch me staring at his girlfriend. She didn't really have much to say."

Orion must have taken that box, placed the bomb in it, and then sent his girlfriend to plant it on that man's truck at some point.

Cassidy's stomach turned as she pictured it playing out, as she began to understand just how devious his whole plan was.

She stepped closer, a new fire burning in her gut.

"Jimmy James, did you give this man information about us?"

He didn't say anything.

There was more than Jimmy James was telling them. His shifty gaze said it all.

Ty leaned closer and growled, "Answer the lady's question."

He ran a hand over his face, pausing at his forehead. His eyes scrunched shut, as if he was in pain. "He may have asked a couple of questions about you. Like where you liked to hang out. Who your friends were. When I'd seen you last."

"And you answered them?" Ty's voice held an edge of unmistakable disgust and disbelief.

"He slipped me some extra money," Jimmy James said. "I knew I should keep my mouth shut, but . . ."

"I'm disappointed in you," Ty said. "But I'll deal with that later. Right now, we've got to find Serena."

Ty stormed away, his shoulders tight, his steps fast, and his gaze simmering. Cassidy had never seen this side of him before. She scrambled to keep up with him.

"I can't believe he would do this," Ty muttered.

"I can't either. But when this is done, you can talk to him again. Ty, I realized something."

He paused. When he glanced at her, some of the anger drained from his face.

"Orion knew about the ferry, yet he wasn't in the crowds."

"Okay."

"He's obviously somewhere he can watch all of this play out," Cassidy said.

"The lighthouse." Realization spread across his features. "Let's go."

———

Cassidy's pulse spiked as they sped away from the marina. This could be it. This could be where Orion was keeping Serena.

Please, God, let her be there. Let her be okay. Keep Ty and Mac safe.

"We need a plan for when we get there," Cassidy said.

"We take him by surprise," Mac said.

They'd updated him when they climbed into the truck.

"I agree," Ty said. "We can park to the side of the road before we reach the lighthouse and stay concealed in the trees."

"If he's watching from the lighthouse, he'll see us coming," Cassidy reminded them.

"If we come around the east side, there's more cover," Ty said. "We just have to make it a hundred yards or so to reach the building. It's still risky, but doable."

Mac leaned forward on the bench seat and glanced at both of them. "We could create some type of distraction so he's not looking."

"Like what?" Cassidy wasn't sure she liked the glimmer in his eyes.

"I have a flashbang," he said, pulling something from his pocket. "I could throw it out on the other side of the structure while you two go inside."

"Do you always carry one of those with you?" Ty asked.

"Not always. Just most of the time."

Ty relaxed his face by shaking his head slightly. "That might work."

"You going to be okay with an explosion?" Mac asked.

PTSD, Cassidy realized. It had to affect Ty in ways she didn't even know and couldn't even comprehend.

"I've been through one explosion already today and one chase through the water," Ty said. "I'd say I'm well on my way to reliving my days as a SEAL. And, yes, I'm okay."

Cassidy let them talk. Both were more qualified with the tactical side of this. She'd been good at tracking down clues and interrogating suspects, but she'd never trained for SWAT-type missions.

"Cassidy and I will storm the lighthouse," Ty said. "We both have guns. We'll try to catch Orion off guard. Our first priority has to be finding Serena."

"Absolutely," Cassidy said. "We can't do anything that puts her in danger."

"I'll stay back," Mac said. "And I can take them off guard if we need to. Or call for backup. Not Bozeman. But maybe that detective from NCSBI. Dan Peterson."

"Both of you, please be careful," Cassidy's voice wavered. "This is my mess, and I'll never forgive myself if either of you are hurt because of me."

"Your mess is our mess." Mac winked. "That's how family works."

Her heart warmed for a moment. She liked the sound of that. Family.

But she still hated the fact that she'd brought the trouble here with her.

Ty pulled to a stop on the side of the road and coasted his truck into the woods. The branch cover over this part of the road should have concealed them this far—in the best-case scenario, at least.

"Let's do this," Mac said. "I'll see you both at the end of this—with Serena safe and sound. Got it?"

"Got it," Ty said.

Mac took off through one side of the woods, and Ty and Cassidy through the other. Ty took her hand, leading her through the thick brush. He stopped about ten feet in.

"There's his SUV," he said. "Orion is here, Cassidy."

Her heart pounded harder. "At least we know we're on the right track."

"I know you have a lot on your shoulders right now," Ty said as they moved through the foliage.

"Thanks for helping me carry it."

"Anytime, sweetheart. Anytime."

She smiled briefly, knowing he meant the words. And knowing that meant the world to her. When they were through with this, they needed to have a long talk.

She wanted to know about the fleeting doubt she'd seen in his eyes. But there would be time for that later.

She hoped.

A few minutes later, they paused.

They'd reached the edge of the woods.

Cassidy looked up at the towering lighthouse in the distance. Was Orion up there?

The glare of the sun against the glass made it impossible to tell. But she'd bet on him being here.

From the other side of the beach, a blatant reflection signaled to them that Mac had arrived.

Ty took his cell phone and sent a flash of light back to him.

"It's showtime, Cassidy," he said.

She nodded and gripped her gun as a huge bang exploded on the other side of the lighthouse.

WITHOUT WASTING ANY TIME, Cassidy and Ty rushed to the lightkeeper's quarters—and the entrance to the lighthouse. Ty took one side of the front door, and Cassidy took the other. Before opening it, Cassidy glanced in the window.

She saw nothing. No one. Just the dusty old living room.

But that didn't really surprise her—Orion was smarter than that. Cassidy had known he was intelligent, but the way he'd planned this down to the last detail sent chills up her spine.

Ty nodded at her, signaling it was time.

She braced herself. Ty reached for the door and twisted the knob.

To her surprise, it opened. Unlocked.

Was this a trap? She'd be wise to keep that in mind.

Ty slipped inside first, and Cassidy followed.

The living room area they'd stepped into was empty, just as she suspected.

Ty nodded toward the back of the building, where the door to the lighthouse was.

They'd check out the rooms on the way there. Maybe—just maybe—Serena was in one of them.

Slowly and methodically, they moved down the hallway. Quietly and carefully, they opened each door. Stealthily and thoroughly, they searched each room.

No Serena.

Was she at the top of the lighthouse with Orion? It was a possibility. If that was the case, exactly what was Orion planning? Cassidy's stomach twisted at the thought.

They stepped back into the hallway and finally reached the door at the end. The heavy door that was kept locked, the one leading to the tower.

Ty tugged on it. It opened with a gentle creak.

They glanced at each other.

It was a possibility that Orion may not have heard it if the wind was howling from up above. They wouldn't know unless they kept going.

As soon as they entered, a figure stepped from behind the staircase, gun drawn and aimed at Cassidy.

It wasn't Orion.

It wasn't Serena.

No, it was . . .

"Rose?" Cassidy croaked, staring at the woman in disbelief.

Rose Alvarez. The woman who'd been abducted by

human traffickers. The woman Cassidy had saved, risking her life to do so.

But she wasn't back in Charleston trying to make a better life for herself. No, she was here.

And she obviously wasn't offering an extended thank-you by assisting Cassidy. No, she was the mystery woman who'd been with Orion.

She was on the opposite side of this fight.

———

Rose shook her head, still gripping her gun without any sign of nerves shaking her limbs or voice.

"I'm sorry, Cassidy," she muttered, only her lips moving. Her teeth appeared clenched and tight.

"What . . . How . . ." Cassidy hardly had the words to say.

"It's a long story," Rose muttered, as tense as a cat about to pounce. "But I need you both to put down your weapons."

"You do realize there are two of us and one of you," Ty's gaze remained on Rose's gun. He could take her. No doubt about it. But the move would be risky.

"Of course I do! But if you hurt me, your little friend dies. End of story. So I'd think twice about trying anything funny." She sneered.

Was Rose on something? That would be Cassidy's guess. Not flakka. But she didn't appear to be in her right mind.

The thought caused a surge of sadness in Cassidy.

The woman had been given a second chance at life . . . and this was how she was using it? What a waste. And a shame.

"Okay," Cassidy said. She exchanged a look with Ty, and he nodded.

Slowly, they both lowered their guns to the stone floor.

Rose had meant the words, and they couldn't take any chances. Not when someone else's life was on the line.

"Now we just need to wait a few minutes," Rose said. "Right here. Close the door," she instructed.

Ty closed it, but his eyes kept going to her gun, as if formulating a plan.

What if they took her out? How would Orion know? Was he even here still? How were the two communicating?

The next few minutes would be precarious, at best.

"How did you get involved with this, Rose?" Cassidy asked, unsure why they had to wait. Unsure if she wanted to know. But she did want answers. Desperately.

Some of the hardness left her eyes. "I'm sorry, Cassidy. I never meant to do this. But I needed money."

"What do I have to do with money?" Cassidy asked.

And why was everyone willing to sell their souls for some cash? Was wealth really that much of a god? She knew the answer—yes. But desperation could also motivate people to do despicable things. It was a different kind of idol.

"Someone came into town." Rose's breathing appeared more labored now—fast, shallow breaths. Her voice softened slightly, and a thin layer of sweat formed on her lip. "I started running around with the wrong crowd. This guy was using his connections, trying to find someone."

"Okay . . ."

"He had a picture of you. Or someone who looked like you. I realized that you were the same woman wanted by DH-7. The man saw the recognition on my face. He was going to kill me if I didn't give him the information. I just knew. I had to work with him. I had no other choice."

This wasn't the time to lecture her about how people always had a choice. Cassidy understood now more than ever just how hard it could be.

"So you led him here?" Ty didn't bother to hide the surprise and disgust from his voice. First Jimmy James. Now Rose. Betrayal was never easy to swallow.

"I tried to misdirect him at first. He did this." She raised her sleeve and revealed a large gash in her arm. "I had to, Cassidy. I had to."

"You can walk away now," Cassidy said, staring at the gun. Time was ticking away. "You can choose your ending."

"But I can't. He's going to give me a hundred K if I help him."

Cassidy's stomach twisted. "You're going to choose money over the right thing?"

"I need the cash." Her voice trembled. "I know it sounds horrible, but I do. It could change my life."

"Don't do this, Rose," Ty said. "There are better ways. More honest ways."

Footsteps sounded on the stairway. Orion was coming. When he got his hands on her, Cassidy's life would be over.

Would Serena finally be safe? Or would he kill her too? Along with Ty?

Please, Lord . . .

One more step, and Orion appeared. A smug grin stretched across his face as he pointed his gun at her.

"If it isn't Cady," he muttered. "I can't tell you how long I've dreamed of this day."

TWENTY-FOUR

"YOU DON'T HAVE to bring anyone else into this, Orion," Cassidy said. Her stomach curled at the sight of him, at the arrogant expression on his face and his cocky movement. This was the real Orion. Baggy clothes. Exposed tattoos. Urban dialect.

All planned. Precise. Deadly.

"Oh, but I do. Do you realize how many of my friends you made suffer?"

"I didn't make them suffer," she said. "They were involved with a deadly gang, and they made their choices."

He'd stopped five steps above the floor, high enough —and far enough—that they couldn't reach him. And his gun was aimed at Ty, while Rose's was pointed at Cassidy.

There was no easy way out of this.

And there was still no sign of Serena. Time wasn't on their side right now.

"Where's Serena?" Cassidy asked. "She has nothing to do with this."

"Wouldn't you like to know?" Orion smiled, finding a sick satisfaction in holding the power of suffering in his hands. "That's my little secret."

"Let her go," Ty said. "We can figure it out another way."

He chuckled. "Did you know your girlfriend stopped my friend Raul's heart? I'm sure I can think of a way to make your heart stop as well so she can know how it feels."

"No!" Cassidy felt the blood leaving her face at the mere mention of it. "You just want me. Leave him alone."

"You'll have to go through me to get to her," Ty growled.

"That could be fun," Orion said.

Cassidy couldn't stomach the thought of it. "What was with all the pretense, Orion? Why'd you catch us in the church parking lot? Why are you drawing this out?"

"Part of the enjoyment is watching you suffer. Watching your confusion and doubt. Watching you try to figure out if I was really the man you once knew or someone else. I've always been fascinated by you, Cady."

Her stomach churned as a brief image of the kiss he'd forced on her flashed in her mind. In an instant, she remembered his pungent smell, the repulsive feel of his chapped lips pressing against hers. But she needed to turn this conversation around before Orion got in her head.

"Who'd you tell I was here?" she asked.

"No one, of course. I want the money for myself. The satisfaction of knowing I did what no one else could. The gang members back home . . . they're like a bunch of starved prisoners who are desperate for something to eat and gnaw on. If I turned them loose, this whole place would become crack town for a while."

She pushed down a shiver at the image. Her gut clenched. She'd only taken one life, and it was Raul's. Even though he was a bad guy, it would haunt her for the rest of her life. "What are you doing, Orion? What do you want with me?"

His cocky grin turned into a sneer. "I'm going to make you pay, just as I promised. You want to know something else strange? One of my cohorts saw Reginald the other day. It turns out he didn't die. You have a strange habit of having that happen around you."

At least Cassidy knew he was okay. Momentary comfort filled her.

"There are better ways than death," she said.

"Unless it came to Raul?"

"He wasn't supposed to die. It was an accident."

Like a switch had flipped, his playfulness turned to vengeance. "Sure, it was. Tie up your friend."

Cassidy glanced at Ty, her heart pounding in her ears. "No, I'm not tying him up."

"I don't think you understand. You're not the one calling the shots here. Tie him up."

"I don't even have anything to tie him up with."

"Rose?"

Rose reached into her pocket and pulled out some handcuffs. She tossed them to Cassidy.

"Do it," Orion ordered. "Or I shoot him."

Images of what might happen to Ty filled her head. All of them ended with him dead. The situation felt no-win. She hesitated.

Orion raised his gun, pointing it at Ty. "I said, do it, and do it now!"

Rose stepped forward. "Can't I just do it? Let's just make this easy."

"Yes, let's make it easy." As soon as Orion said the words, his gun fired.

Cassidy held her breath, waiting for the pain. Devastation. Loss.

Rose collapsed to the floor.

Cassidy gasped and sank down beside her. "Rose!"

Blood soaked her shoulder, and she moaned. Her eyes glazed, and shock froze her expression. She wouldn't make it long, not without help.

"Now, did I make myself clear?" Orion said. "Handcuff him."

"You could have killed her!" Cassidy glanced up at Orion. "She was on your side."

"I was going to kill her either way. She was stupid enough to believe I'd split any money with her."

"It's okay, Cassidy," Ty said. "I'll be okay."

Her hands trembled as she stood and picked up the handcuffs.

What if Orion got angry and shot Ty? She couldn't live with that image in mind.

Ty put his hands together in front of him, desperately trying to tell her something with his gaze. Cassidy wasn't sure what.

She snapped the cuffs around his wrists.

"I'm sorry," she whispered, wanting more than anything to turn back time. To go back a few days to when she'd been floating on the clouds with happiness.

She should have known it wouldn't last.

"It's okay," Ty told her. "I love you, Cassidy."

Emotions lodged in her throat upon hearing the words again. "I love you too, Ty."

Orion rushed down the steps and grabbed Ty by the shoulder.

Cassidy shouted and tried to push him away. It was no use.

Ty threw his elbow into Orion's throat. Orion gawked but quickly righted himself. He grabbed Cassidy and put the gun to her head.

"I'd stop if I were you," Orion growled.

Ty raised his hands. "I stopped. Don't hurt her."

"Step into the hallway."

Ty seemed to freeze. "Why don't you take me instead of Cassidy?"

"Cassidy is the only one I want." He pressed the gun so hard that Cassidy let out a cry. "Now, step out. Now."

"Okay, okay." Ty gave Cassidy one last look—one that was full of apology and regret.

As soon as Ty was in the hallway, Orion slammed the door and bolted it shut, barricading them from the rest of the world.

She could hardly stomach the fact.

Orion turned back toward Cassidy with that gleam in his gaze again. "Now it's time for you and me to have some fun."

———

Cassidy felt like she'd stepped outside herself as Orion led her up the lighthouse stairs. She nearly stumbled on the steps. She could hardly breathe.

They'd come this far only for this. No Serena to be found, Rose was dying, Ty would live the rest of his life in guilt, and Cassidy was breathing her final moments.

A mental countdown started again. Only she wasn't sure when this clock would stop.

"You don't have to do this," she said.

He shoved her onto the catwalk. "Of course I do. You're going to set an example. Just like Reginald was supposed to. Remember?"

"I do." The wind whipped around them, so strong that she pressed herself against the glass of the lantern room. She sucked in a breath. This glass was strong. It would hold her.

She glanced back. If it didn't, it was a long way down. What had Ty said? Eleven stories?

She forced her eyes ahead instead. The water had turned ugly within the last few hours as the tide came in. What had she heard on the news earlier? That the mixture of an offshore storm and a full moon was going to bring an unusually high tide. That looked true now. The water was probably ten feet higher inland.

"The strange thing is, everyone you supposedly killed is turning up alive," Orion said. "Why is that?"

"Zombie apocalypse?" Why had Cassidy said that? It was too late to take it back now.

Orion chuckled, but it sounded dry and bitter. "Aren't you funny? Raul was certainly taken with you. That's what ultimately got him killed."

"Raul was evil."

The gun slammed into Cassidy's face, knocking the wind out of her.

"Shut up! Raul was a good man."

She grabbed her aching jaw, trying to alleviate the pain. "What did he ever do that was so good? He looked out for only one person—Raul. He only wanted to make himself richer."

"He looked out for all of us." Spittle hit her face.

"You're a fool if that's what you think," Cassidy said. "What did he ever do for you?"

"He gave me a place to stay. Money. A purpose."

She inched around the lighthouse, trying to calculate if she could run. How far she could get down the steps before his bullet would find her? Before she tumbled? And this escape became a suicide mission.

"I think your loyalty is misguided," she said. "Unless there's someone else. Who's paying you?"

An honest grin crossed his face. "You really don't know, do you?"

"Know what?"

He laughed again. "Raul was never the one calling all the shots, holding all the money."

Realization swept through her like the aftershock of a nuclear bomb. "Who is it?"

"I can't tell."

"Why not? You're going to kill me anyway."

"Because you don't deserve to know. You deserve to die." He stared at her and shook his head. "You think you're so smart. You're not."

"You have no conscience."

"Shut up!" He raised his gun and pulled the trigger.

CHAPTER
TWENTY-FIVE

CASSIDY GRABBED her arm as pain sliced through her. She glanced down, expecting the worst. It appeared the bullet had skimmed her arm. A flesh wound.

But she knew Orion was just getting started. That wasn't a mistake. It was a sign of things to come.

"Raul trusted you," Orion said, aiming his gun at her. "How could you have done this to him?"

"Raul was a twisted man. Just like you." Probably not the best thing Cassidy could say right now, but she may as well speak the truth. It wouldn't make a difference to the outcome either way.

Warm liquid covered her fingers, but she didn't dare look. The sight of it would only make her lightheaded—the last thing she needed up here.

"People like me have been discounted for too long," Orion snapped. "We were the uprising, giving the power back to the right people."

"You wanted power for your own gain," she said. "You weren't in this to help anyone but yourselves."

"Still mouthy, I see. Let's see if I can put an end to this. You're not as much fun as I'd thought you'd be. In fact, you're giving me a headache."

Still holding his gun, he reached down and grabbed something. Was that a . . . noose?

"Put it on," he barked.

No way was Cassidy putting that thing around her neck. She'd die fighting first.

She dashed to the other side of the lantern room atop the lighthouse. Running in circles wasn't ideal—but it was something.

Orion yelled out an obscenity before coming after her.

After one circuit, they both paused. Cassidy could see him on the other side of the glass, casting her a death glare.

She tried to catch her breath and gripped her arm. If she was going down, she wasn't going to make it easy for him.

He lunged toward her again, and she took off around the cylinder. She could go down the stairs. But she'd be an open target if she did.

Think, Cassidy. Think.

But she was out of good ideas. Out of Day-at-a-Glance wisdom.

She had nothing.

Her breathing came in short gasps, and her head spun. Orion suddenly stopped and changed directions.

She pivoted to turn, but her foot caught on something, and she crashed onto the metal grate below her.

Her heart pounding in her ears, she glanced up. Saw Orion coming toward her, a crazed smirk on his face.

This was it. He was going to put that noose around her neck, and this was all going to be over.

It's been a good run, God. But this isn't the way it's supposed to end.

"You always have to make things complicated," Orion said.

Just as the words left his mouth, the wind kicked up. It wasn't just any wind—it was probably a forty-mile-an-hour gust.

The breeze caught Orion off guard. His eyes widened, and he stepped back to catch his balance.

His heel hit the edge of the catwalk. He started to fall backward, into the railing.

But the metal support groaned. Ty had warned her about that section, hadn't he? Said it was loose.

Orion's eyes widened. His arms windmilled as he grabbed the air, trying to catch himself.

But it was too late.

He fell from the catwalk.

Cassidy closed her eyes, waiting for the inevitable moment when he hit the ground. It came with a sickening thud.

She should have caught him.

No, she realized.

Orion would have only pulled her down with him. They both would have died.

She glanced at the ground below and saw police cars had arrived.

Rose.

Someone needed to get to Rose and help her before it was too late.

No one could get through that barricade Orion set up.

Cassidy rushed down the steps and found the woman on the dirty floor. Blood pooled around her, and little gasps escaped from her lips.

Cassidy knelt beside her. "Rose, it's going to be okay. Help is almost here."

"Cassidy . . ." she whispered.

Cassidy leaned closer. "I'm here."

"I didn't tell anyone else . . . you were here," she whispered. "I'm sorry . . . this happened."

"You just worry about getting better."

"I shouldn't have . . ."

"It's okay." Cassidy's mental clock started ticking again. Rose needed help. Now. "But I need to open the door."

"Cassidy . . ." she whispered again. "Your friend is close. She's . . . not far. Get her before the tide rises."

"Where? Can you tell me where?"

"Moon . . ." she muttered.

Then Rose's eyes closed.

She was gone, Cassidy realized.

Moisture filled her eyes. Maybe Rose had held on just long enough to tell Cassidy that. But Cassidy had held so much hope Rose would change, that she'd take that second chance. Instead, she'd given in and sold herself in order to belong. In order to gain money.

In the end, Rose had redeemed herself. She'd taken a bullet for them. At least there was something to be said for that.

"Cassidy, are you in there?" Someone banged on the door, reminding her that it wasn't too late.

She rushed toward it and unbolted it.

Ty rushed inside and pulled her into his arms as paramedics flooded the space.

"Are you okay?" Ty asked, pressing her face between his hands. The police must have been able to get his handcuffs off.

"Yes, but . . ." She looked at her arm and saw the blood there. Then she looked at Rose, and her knees felt weak.

"I've got you, sweetheart. I've got you."

Her head spun a moment, yet her brain wouldn't stop working. "Where's Mac?"

"I'm right here." He stepped in behind them. "He's gone, Cassidy. He . . . didn't survive the fall."

She swallowed hard, remembering every detail. "Maybe this lighthouse was looking out for me," Cassidy said.

"Maybe another kind of lighthouse was," Ty said.

"Amen." Her smile faded. "Mac, I need you to do something for me."

"Anything."

"Rose told me Serena was close. I don't know where,

but she's not inside this lighthouse. Rose suggested Serena's near the water and then she muttered 'moon.'"

"The August Moon," Ty said.

Cassidy's breath caught. "Yes, that's got to be it. It makes sense. And the tide is rising. The boat is going to be covered soon."

"I'm on it," Mac said.

Ty slipped his arm around Cassidy. "We'll get you fixed up. I'm just grateful you're alive."

She buried herself in his chest. "I'm glad you're okay. This . . . this could have turned out much differently."

"Yes, it could have."

TWENTY-SIX

CASSIDY STOOD beside the lighthouse wrapped in a blanket—not to ward away the cold since it was still hot outside. She wore it to protect her from the sand the strong winds blasted through the air. She used it as a small symbol of comfort.

A paramedic had cleaned her wounds. Bandaged her temple and arm. Tried to take her to the clinic. She'd refused. Ty remained glued to her side the entire time.

But the person she most wanted to see right now was Serena. It had been fifteen minutes. Where was Mac? Was he okay? What had Orion done to Serena? The questions pummeled her until Cassidy could hardly breathe.

Finally, two figures emerged from around a bend of trees.

"Is that them?" Cassidy asked, everything else fading from around her.

"I think so."

She let out a cry of relief. Serena's look today wasn't purposeful. Her hair was messy, her skin pale, her clothes dirty. But she was alive, which meant this might be her best look of all.

Cassidy started to step toward her when Skye's car squealed toward the end of the road, braking so hard the vehicle's nose dipped toward the ground. She threw her car in Park and ran across the sand to her niece. The two embraced. Cassidy gave them some time together, not wanting to ruin the moment.

As she waited, Bozeman strode toward them from the lighthouse.

A glint of cynicism filled his gaze as it hit Cassidy. "You two want to explain how you're involved in this?"

Ty started to speak, but Cassidy stopped him. She didn't want other people to carry the weight of her problems, not when she was capable. "It's my fault. That man is someone from my past. I never expected him to show up here in Lantern Beach. From the moment I saw him, I knew he'd bring trouble."

"Why didn't you tell me that trouble came into town?"

She pulled the blanket tighter. "I had no proof. Just my observations. I figured it wouldn't do any good."

"So was this all about you?" Bozeman continued to stare. Of all the times he chose to have some common sense, it had to be now.

"This was all about him," Cassidy said. "He may have come here to find me, but what he really wanted was to expand his criminal enterprise. His drug reach. That's what he does. He saw Lantern Beach as a target."

"That doesn't explain the bomb or why he grabbed your friend."

"Drugs do crazy things to people," Cassidy said, hoping he bought that explanation. It was true—just incomplete. "He wasn't in his right mind."

"I'm going to have to take your word on that. He can't speak for himself." A shadow of doubt crossed his face.

"I'm sure the autopsy will answer a lot," Ty said, his arm tightening around Cassidy.

"I'm hoping it will," Bozeman said. "And you said the wind pushed him off?"

"That's right. I've been preoccupied for the past few days, and I didn't even watch the weather. Apparently, he didn't either because he didn't anticipate Mother Nature being an obstacle."

"The high winds today are a doozy. There's also a small craft advisory and the risk of ocean overwash as well."

"Well, it worked in my favor today. I'm thankful for that."

"I see." Bozeman nodded slowly. "We may have more questions. Stay in town."

"You know where to find us."

As soon as Bozeman walked away, Serena broke away from the detective she was speaking with and ran toward Cassidy.

"I'm so sorry," Serena muttered, throwing her arms

around Cassidy and sobbing. "I should have taken the ice cream truck back when you told me. But I thought it would help us both out if I could sell more. I was so stupid."

"Don't worry about it," Cassidy said. "I'm just glad you're okay."

Serena stared off at the water and wiped her moist eyes. "I didn't think anyone was going to find me. Thank you for sending Mac."

"He went on his own." Cassidy studied her tear-stained face a moment. "I know we don't have much time right now, but what happened?"

"Elsa started playing 'Who Let the Dogs Out?' Who would have thought?" She let out a sardonic laugh.

"You didn't program that song?" Ty asked.

Serena shook her head. "No, I have no idea how to. And people started rushing toward the truck to get their free ice cream sandwiches I'd promised. I . . . uh . . . I ran out. I'll buy more. So sorry."

"Don't worry about that now."

"Anyway, a man approached. I didn't even recognize him, Cassidy. I'd seen his picture, but it didn't register. He seemed nice when he asked for ice cream and told me I was pretty. The next thing I knew, he held a gun. Told me to get out and follow him or he'd kill me."

Cassidy's heart throbbed with compassion and regret. "I'm sorry that happened to you, Serena."

Serena hugged her again. "Thanks again for finding me."

A detective came and told Serena they had more questions. She nodded at Cassidy and Ty before reluctantly going to speak with more law enforcement, and this was just beginning. The police would have endless questions for everyone involved here.

Skye sauntered over. The woman swallowed hard, her movements tight with tension. "I guess I owe you an apology too," she said.

Cassidy touched Skye's arm, trying to pull her out of the vortex of regret that seemed to drag her under. "No, you don't. You were scared."

The wind blew her long, untamed hair in her face and billowed out her flowy ankle-length skirt. "I shouldn't have taken it out on you. I've just . . . I've been stabbed in the back before. I think the worst of people sometimes, and I let my emotions get the best of me. Please forgive me."

"Of course," Cassidy said. "That's what friends do."

They hugged. Friends, Cassidy mused. It felt so good to be surrounded by them now.

———

Mac joined them several minutes later. Cassidy expected him to look relieved, maybe even giddy at the outcome. Instead, his posture was tense, and all the normal mischief was gone from his gaze.

"What's going on?" Ty seemed to sense Mac's mood as well, based on the hardness of his voice and the way his muscles suddenly bristled.

"There's been something bothering me about that bomb," Mac said, lowering his voice and glancing around. "I just realized what it was."

"Please share." Cassidy's pulse spiked with anticipation. She had no idea where he was going with this, but she could tell this would be no laughing matter.

Mac scanned everything around him one more time. "Before I retired as police chief, one of my last cases involved a husband who left his wife in her rental house with a bomb."

"Okay . . ." Cassidy said.

"That bomb is the one from the evidence locker at the police station," Mac said.

Cassidy blinked. She couldn't have heard correctly. The bomb was from an earlier crime that had been committed on the island? "Come again?"

Mac nodded. "I can't prove it. But I know it's the same one. Of course, we didn't leave the bomb in there assembled. But we left enough of it together that a person would only have to add a few things to make it deadly again."

Ty shifted, his hands going to his hips. "So does this mean what I'm thinking it means?"

Mac leveled his gaze with them. "It means, there may be a dirty cop on the force here in Lantern Beach."

Cassidy's head swirled. She'd suspected someone on the force might be involved in some late-night drug deals. But she'd had bigger issues at hand than checking into that. Maybe it should have been more of a priority.

"What are you going to do about it?" Ty asked.

Mac rubbed his beard and stared off into the distance a moment. "Nothing—for now. But I'm going to keep my eyes open. Orion obviously found out about the area's less-than-savory characters easily. They must have connected him to everyone he needed to know here to enable his plan."

The thought wasn't comforting to Cassidy. But, like Mac said, that was going to be a problem for another day. Right now, she needed to rest and revel in the fact that she'd lived to see another day.

Cassidy and Ty didn't reach their cottages until after dark. They'd been questioned again before they left the scene at the lighthouse, and Cassidy had managed to hide from the police her true identity.

Without Orion or Rose there to tell their side, her secret was safe . . . for a while, at least. But the fact remained that Cassidy had solved too many cases, been involved in too much. And when they learned Orion was part of DH-7, who knew what might happen?

But for now, Cassidy just needed to breathe.

She and Ty sat in their favorite spot—the swing on his porch. Kujo jumped up beside them and laid his head in Cassidy's lap. It was too dark outside to see the ocean, but they could hear the swells pounding the shore. Crickets and frogs offered their soundtracks around them as well, and the steady breeze of the wind felt refreshing and served as a reminder that everything was okay.

For now.

She wished she could say the same for Rose. She wished the woman had another chance at redemption. But her final act had been selfless. Cassidy grieved the loss yet felt entirely grateful that the woman who'd led Orion to her had ultimately helped to save Serena's life.

Cassidy leaned into Ty, careful to avoid rubbing her wounds against him. Ty's shoulder was probably going to be sore tomorrow, although he denied it. Cassidy hoped he hadn't undone all the progress he'd made since his surgery.

"Orion told me there's someone else in charge of DH-7," Cassidy said after a few moments of silence.

Ty tensed beside her. "What do you mean?"

"I figured Orion was the one calling all the shots since Raul died. But, according to him, there's always been someone else. All the money is channeled through this person."

"Do you have any idea who?"

Cassidy rubbed Kujo's head. The dog seemed to sense the danger they'd been in and hadn't left their sides since they got back. "No, I don't. I have a feeling the FBI doesn't either."

"Did you tell Samuel—isn't that your contact's name?"

"It is. And I haven't. But what if it's Samuel?"

Ty didn't say anything for a minute. "He would have just sent someone to kill you, right?"

"Not if he doesn't want the finger pointed at him." Cassidy released a sigh. Things felt even more complicated now instead of simpler, like she'd hoped they might. "I really have no idea. No clue at all. But I don't like the thought of someone else being at the reins. DH-7 needs to dissolve."

"Answers will come to light in time."

She frowned. "My fear is how they'll come to light."

"However it happens, I'll be beside you." He kissed the top of her head.

"Thank you, Ty."

Silence fell around them as they swayed back and forth. Cassidy's thoughts swirled inside her. The events of the past few days were a lot to comprehend and would take a while to mentally sort through. And hiding her real identity was going to become harder than ever.

She worried about the videos people had filmed when those surfers had taken flakka and unleashed themselves on the boardwalk. If they went viral, would someone recognize her? She'd been wearing a hat and sunglasses.

But still.

Maybe if she truly kept a low profile over the next few months, she'd still be able to pull this off.

And maybe she and Ty really would have a chance at a future together.

She turned to him, her heart swelling with love again. "You want to tell me why you've been so melancholy?"

He laced his fingers through hers, his expression pensive. "I realized that you might not stick around here, and I can't stand the thought of losing you."

"Why would you lose me?"

"Your dad is one of the wealthiest men in the country. You're a detective. You have a good life far away from here."

"Not really, Ty." She frowned. "Listen, I don't know what the future holds. I tried to tell you that from the start. My life is back in Seattle. I would never ask you to move there."

"And it would seem a shame if I asked you to stay in a place as small as Lantern Beach."

She ran her hand along the side of his face, tracing the edges, relishing the view. "What's that Scripture? Don't worry about tomorrow for tomorrow will worry about itself?"

"Yeah, that's the one. You're right." He breathed out a laugh. "I would never want you to stay here unless it was something you wanted, Cassidy. Island life isn't for everyone. And I don't have much to offer. Definitely not money. Or status. Or even a nice home."

"I don't need those things, Ty. I've been there and done that. It's been my life. And you know what? My parents aren't any happier because of what they have. I'm grateful that I realized that at a relatively young age."

He squeezed her hand. "That's good to know."

She shifted, pulling her leg beneath her so she could look Ty in the eye. "My best friend, Lucy, used to be a little boy crazy. There was nothing she loved to talk about more than cute guys and getting married one day. She had her entire wedding planned out, right down to the flavor of her cake. Almond, by the way."

"Okay . . ." A wrinkle formed between his eyes.

"Stick with me. I'm going somewhere with this. I promise. One thing she always said stuck with me. She used to say that she hoped to marry a tender warrior."

"A tender warrior?"

Cassidy nodded. "I never really understood what that meant. I mean, guys who are tough aren't usually the sensitive type. And the sensitive men usually aren't tough. Then I met you."

A smile tugged at his lips. "I like where this is going."

"Suddenly, the words made perfect sense, and I totally get what she was talking about. Like I said, I don't know what the future holds. But I'm trusting that God has a plan for you and me. Hopefully for you and me together. And as soon as the trial is over, we'll figure that out. Until then, my hands are tied. I'm at the mercy of the justice system."

"You are getting good at this whole sweet talk thing," Ty said.

The warmth of his voice curled around, making her feel as cozy as her favorite blanket. "You make it easy."

"See? Listen to you now."

She laughed. But the sound was cut short when his lips covered hers.

~~~

Thank you for reading *Dangerous Waters*. If you enjoyed this book, please consider leaving a review.

Keep reading for a preview of *Perilous Riptide*.
~~~

AVAILABLE NOW:
PERILOUS RIPTIDE

PERILOUS RIPTIDE: CHAPTER ONE

TODAY'S GOALS: FIX ELSA.
LEARN HOW TO COOK SHRIMP
SCAMPI. WATCH THE SUNSET.

CASSIDY LIVINGSTON LEANED against one of the thick wooden posts that held her tiny beach cottage high off the sandy ground. After giving Kujo—an adorably sweet golden retriever with an unfortunate name—a pat on the head, she sighed. She never thought she'd get this much enjoyment from doing nothing.

Across from her, her neighbor Ty pulled apart her ice cream truck, Elsa.

The bright pink truck with the hand-scribbled prices had needed some work for a while, but with the busy summer season, Cassidy hadn't wanted the vehicle to be out of commission for too long. Labor Day weekend had just ended, which meant that tourists here on Lantern Beach would trickle back to their homes and their jobs and bide their time until they could experience another vacation in paradise.

Cassidy's throat went dry as she watched Ty, and she took another long sip of her lemonade. Her dad had always been more of an inside person—a filthy rich businessman, for that matter. He paid people to do everything for him except get him dressed.

But Ty . . . he was another breed of man. He was handy, he didn't mind sweat or dirt, and he looked good throughout it all. Really good.

Right now, his white T-shirt clung to his defined muscles. A sheen of moisture covered his skin, screaming of hard work. His eyes looked determined and focused. The former Navy SEAL was inarguably the man of Cassidy's dreams.

She took another long sip of her icy lemonade.

"Can you hand me that adjustable wrench?" Ty raised his head just enough to project his voice through the humidity-laden island air.

Like a dutiful helper, Cassidy found what he was looking for in his well-used tool chest and brought it to him. "As you wish."

He breathed out a laugh and glanced at her. "You sound so compliant."

"I am." Her voice lilted teasingly.

"Of course you are." He chuckled again, not hiding his obvious doubt.

They both knew that Cassidy was stubborn and headstrong. As a detective in Seattle, she'd had to be both of those things at times. Then again, her life as Cady Matthews seemed so far away.

Cassidy kind of liked the new person she'd become —the laid-back, let-her-hair-down, enjoy-each-moment kind of person. Maybe it was who she'd always been but had never acknowledged.

Cassidy leaned into the truck, inspecting Ty's work even more closely. He'd removed the dash in an effort to figure out why the vehicle spontaneously began to play music—and usually at the worst times. Cassidy had been woken up many nights by digitized tunes like "My Bonnie Lies over the Ocean" and "Pop! Goes the Weasel." The last song definitely made her want to pop something.

"Well, what do we have here?" Ty reached into the depths of the dash and emerged with some kind of notebook. He stared at the leather cover a moment before handing it to Cassidy. "I'll let you check it out."

Cassidy inspected the outside of the worn pages. Yes, it was a book—of the journal variety, if she had to guess. Strange that it was found behind the dashboard.

"If I had to guess, the book was probably in the glove compartment at one time, and somehow it slipped between some crack, never to be found again," Ty said, as if reading her thoughts.

Cassidy leaned against the truck and opened it, expecting to see a log of gas mileage or ice cream sales or something practical.

Instead, she saw hand-scribbled words. And dates. And paragraph after paragraph of . . . commentary.

She squinted at the date on the first page. The journal had been started five years ago.

Flipping to the back, she paused. The entries had ended last October.

That meant . . . Cassidy's breath caught.

That meant that this journal had to belong to Elsa—the person, not the truck.

Elsa was the previous owner of the ice cream truck, the one whose body had been found in the vehicle. Apparently, she'd fallen, hit her head, and that injury had ultimately led to her untimely death.

A few months later, Cassidy had arrived in town and taken up ownership of the ice cream truck when Elsa's best friend, Ernestine, put the vehicle up for sale.

Cassidy's pulse spiked. She'd been curious about Elsa—the person—and had heard various tales about her around town. Elsa was obviously eccentric and lively, and she liked to have fun. Cassidy had felt a bond with the woman ever since she started driving the truck that was Elsa's namesake.

She started to read the first page from the notebook but paused and glanced at Ty. "Can I read this journal? Or is this too intrusive?"

"Whose is it?" Ty's head was still buried inside the truck as he fiddled with some wires.

"I'm nearly certain it's Elsa's."

He stopped working long enough to sit up and look at Cassidy, a knot forming between his warm brown eyes. "The previous owner?"

"The one and only."

"Well, she's not around anymore. It couldn't hurt if you took a little peek." He winked at her. "I won't tell anyone."

That was all the encouragement she needed. Cassidy opened the book again and scanned the first entry.

We have a naked vacationer here on the island. Goes and stands at his window every morning wearing nothing but his birthday suit. No one wants to see that freak show. Thou art not Mark Wahlberg. Or even his distant cousin, sir. Put some clothes on.

Cassidy snickered. She'd seen some strange tourists while on her ice cream route. But never a naked one, thank goodness.

She skipped to the middle, laughing at Elsa's observations about the town. She wasn't sure why the woman had chosen to write a journal about these things and keep it in her truck. But her stories were fascinating.

The next entry Cassidy landed on regaled:

Met a family today who couldn't stop talking about sea glass. They wanted to find sea glass. Blah, blah, blah. They even got their little girls to call it mermaid poop. How sweet. You know what I call it? Litter. People need to pick up after themselves and not send their trash into the sea, where delusional people will later glamorize it.

Cassidy had never thought of it that way.

Cassidy finally skipped toward the back of the journal. This was really what she wanted to read anyway. What Elsa's final entries were like. After all, some people believed Elsa hadn't died in a tragic accident and that she still haunted this truck.

Cassidy didn't believe in ghosts, but . . . the truck

did exhibit very strange quirks sometimes—so many that the locals wouldn't even eat any ice cream from the vehicle, lest they be "cursed."

Cassidy skimmed the last entry and felt the blood drain from her face. She had to read it twice to make sure she hadn't misunderstood.

"Ty, listen to this." She straightened.

She must have sounded serious because Ty stopped working again and sat up, his full attention on her. "I'm all ears."

No, he was all heart wrapped in appealing muscles. She didn't tell him that, though. Not now, at least.

Cassidy began reading aloud. "I'm sitting outside the nature preserve. I like to come here and take a smoke. Don't tell Ernestine. She doesn't approve. Anyway, I saw a movement in the woods. I didn't think much of it at first, but then I realized there were two men out there. They were arguing, just like those two brothers from The Avengers. One of them forced the other one down one of the trails into the woods. Ten minutes later, I heard a gunshot. Only one man later emerged."

"What?" A knot formed between Ty's eyes again.

Cassidy kept reading. "I was going to leave. I was. But then my ice cream truck started playing a song. She's never done that on her own before. I took off as fast as I could. But I just know he killed that other man. But here's the other thing: the man who emerged was wearing a police uniform. And now I fear I may not make it to see my seventy-fifth birthday."

Cassidy and Ty exchanged a glance. Both of them had suspected for a while that one of the officers here was involved with something shady. But Cassidy had been trying to keep her nose out of things and maintain a low profile.

"It sounds like Elsa was murdered, Ty." Cassidy looked up at him, a fire lighting inside her.

"I've seen that look before."

"What look?"

"The one that's usually a catalyst for getting involved with something otherwise forbidden."

"Being curious is forbidden?"

Ty stepped closer and squeezed her arm. "It's more important now than ever that you remain low-key. I came really close to losing you a few weeks ago, and I don't want to go through that again."

Even though Cassidy had changed her identity, a member of DH-7 had found her here in Lantern Beach and had come to collect his one million-dollar bounty. He was dead now—because of his own mistake—but that didn't mean this was all over.

Ty grabbed the sweaty glass of lemonade Cassidy had brought down for him and took a long drink.

"You and I both know there's a dirty cop in the area," she said. "We don't know the extent of what this person has done, but according to Elsa's journal it sounds like murder."

They'd both seen some suspicious activity near the lighthouse. One of the people involved had been wearing a Lantern Beach police uniform. And then there was the bomb that had been planted on a local ferry—a bomb that had been taken from the police station evidence locker. All that mixed with this journal entry verified their concerns.

"Maybe we should tell Mac and let him handle it," Ty said. "As the town's former police chief, he has a better knack for law enforcement than any of the actual law enforcement here on the island."

Cassidy's lips twisted, but she finally nodded stiffly. "You're right. Maybe we should tell Mac. I just have one question first."

Ty raised his drink for another sip. "What's that?"

"Where's this Preserve Elsa mentioned?"

To continue reading click here

ALSO BY CHRISTY BARRITT:

BOOKS IN THE LANTERN BEACH UNIVERSE

LANTERN BEACH MYSTERIES

The series that started it all! When a notorious gang puts a bounty on Detective Cady Matthews' head, she has no choice but to hide until she can testify at trial. But her temporary home across the country on a remote North Carolina island isn't as peaceful as she initially thinks. Living under the new identity of Cassidy Livingston, she struggles to keep her investigative skills tucked away. One wrong move could lead to both her discovery and her demise.

#1 Hidden Currents
#2 Flood Watch
#3 Storm Surge
#4 Dangerous Waters
#5 Perilous Riptide
#6 Deadly Undertow

LANTERN BEACH ROMANTIC SUSPENSE

Standalone romantic suspense novels that fear a pulse-pounding story centered around beloved Lantern Beach residents.

Tides of Deception
Shadow of Intrigue
Storm of Doubt
Winds of Danger
Rains of Remorse
Torrents of Fear

LANTERN BEACH PD

When a cult moves to Lantern Beach, the whole island is in upheaval. Police Chief Cassidy Chambers must find answers before total chaos erupts.

#1 On the Lookout
#2 Attempt to Locate
#3 First Degree Murder
#4 Dead on Arrival
#5 Plan of Action

LANTERN BEACH BLACKOUT

Join a group of Navy SEALs who've come to Lantern Beach to start a private security firm. But a secret from their past may destroy them.

#1 Dark Water

#2 Safe Harbor

#3 Ripple Effect

#4 Rising Tide

LANTERN BEACH GUARDIANS

During a turbulent storm, a child is found on the beach, washed up from the ocean. Making matters worse—the girl can't speak.

#1 Hide and Seek

#2 Shock and Awe

#3 Safe and Sound

LANTERN BEACH BLACKOUT: THE NEW RECRUITS

Four new recruits join Blackout, but someone is determined to teach them a lesson.

#1 Rocco

#2 Axel

#3 Beckett

#4 Gabe

LANTERN BEACH MAYDAY

Kenzie and Jimmy James work on a luxury yacht chartering a dangerous course.

#1 Run Aground
#2 Dead Reckoning
#3 Tipping Point

LANTERN BEACH CHRISTMAS

Catch up with your favorite Lantern Beach characters as they come together to help the town's beloved police chief.

Silent Night

LANTERN BEACH BLACKOUT: DANGER RISING

A new team is formed to combat a new enemy. The mission puts everyone on the line, and failure will mean certain death.

#1 Brandon
#2 Dylan
#3 Maddox
#4 Titus

BEACH BOUND
BOOKS AND BEANS MYSTERIES

When widow Tali Robinson moves to Lantern Beach to renovate an old oceanfront store and turn it into a bookstore/coffee shop, the last thing she expects to find is a human skeleton hidden within the walls. But her troubles don't stop there, and before long she realizes she doesn't have to dig for trouble, she's bound to run into it.

#1 Bound by Murder

#2 Bound by Disaster

#3 Bound by Mystery

#4 Bound by Trouble

#5 Bound by Mayhem

USA Today has called Christy Barritt's books "scary, funny, passionate, and quirky."

Christy writes both mystery and romantic suspense novels that are clean with underlying messages of faith. Her books have sold more than three million copies and have won the Daphne du Maurier Award for Excellence in Suspense and Mystery, have been twice nominated for the Romantic Times Reviewers' Choice Award, and have finaled for both a Carol Award and Foreword Magazine's Book of the Year.

She is married to her Prince Charming, a man who thinks she's hilarious—but only when she's not trying to be. Christy is a self-proclaimed klutz, an avid music lover who's known for spontaneously bursting into song, and a road trip aficionado.

When she's not working or spending time with her family, she enjoys singing, playing the guitar, and exploring small, unsuspecting towns where people have no idea how accident-prone she is.

Find Christy online at:

www.christybarritt.com

www.facebook.com/christybarritt

www.twitter.com/cbarritt

Sign up for Christy's newsletter to get information on all of her latest releases here: **www.christybarritt.com/ newsletter-sign-up/**

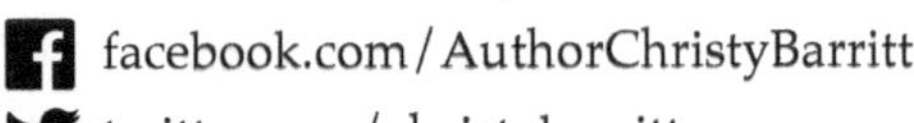